ZERO

Edited by TW Brown

Cover and Design by Shawn Conn

Dedication

This book is dedicated to George A. Romero,
the Patient Zero who infected us all.

Foreward

How did it all begin for you? What was the instant you became a diehard zombophile? For me, it was my fourteenth birthday when a neighbor took me to see *Dawn of the Dead.* The funny thing is, I was actually there to see the other film playing in the double-feature (remember those days?).

So…think back to the past dozen or so zombie books you've read. How many really delve into how it all begins? It has to start somewhere…right? In these pages, you will find out how it all began.

Seven writers have given you a look at that first person to fall: Patient Zero. This anthology opens the door to the genesis of the zombie apocalypse in detail. Could it really be something as simple as a paper cut? The answer awaits you.

As the editor for May December Publications, I welcome you to the anthology that provides the set up for any zombie story you will ever read after.

Where is my good spoon?
TW Brown
August 2011

Contents

The Morning Show Host
By Patrick Shand

This doesn't start like you'd expect. I mean, everyone has read a zombie book or at least seen a zombie flick, right? George Romero is pretty much an essential part of pop culture now, isn't he? The genre of horror is almost synonymous with the image of hordes of the undead lumbering around a town, which, inevitably, is cloaked in thick, thick fog. Turns out, that's not only a staple of the horror genre, but also what I see when I look out the window.

And I started it.

Me. Minnie Brown. You'd think with a name like that I was either destined to become a cartoon mouse or a porn star, but instead I'm the chick that kick-started the end of mankind. To be honest, I'm broken up about it, but that's the last time you're going to read something like that in *this* journal. While this is, in essence, a long-form apology to mankind, it's also the last thing I'll ever write. So I don't want to spend my time here bitching. I figure there must be someone alive out there, and if they find this...well, maybe they'll think, "Hey, that bitch who started all of this zombie apocalypse nonsense? At least she was funny."

So here I go. Here's how, in just one short month, the fictional disease that sold millions of books, B-movies, horror comics got *real*.

It started out with a sale at the library. They were selling these old used books for ten cents each. Granted, they were the books the library was going to throw in the garbage if no one took them, but still. A book for a dime is unbeatable. Well, unless you go on Amazon.com—

sometimes, they sell books for a penny there. A friggin' penny.

I digress.

So I bought this book, a thick one called *Richard Johnson's Dirty Jokes*. It was made up of all these terrible puns and awkward jokes from the sixties or seventies, so I figured it would be a hoot to bring it onto my radio show and read on air. Oh, yeah, I guess that's important. Before all this apocalypse business, I was the host of a morning show on the local radio station. It didn't pay much, but we have the top floor of the building, so while we're up there goofing off, telling jokes, and making prank calls, we've got this beautiful view of the whole town.

In fact, as I write this, I'm sitting in my old chair, looking out at that once breathtaking view. Now it's horrifying. Hundreds, maybe thousands, of things that used to be people are down there, waiting for someone to come out of this building so they can feast. I wonder how many of them used to listen to my show. I wonder how many of them had laughed at my jokes while driving to work in the morning.

Again with the digression. It's hard to keep your mind focused when what you're focusing on is so goddamn bleak.

But I got the book. And that is *really* what started it all; a book full of sexual puns and dick jokes written by a man who called himself Richard Johnson. I leafed through the book while my boyfriend Isaac drove us back to the apartment and, of course, my clumsy ass got a paper cut, one of those painful ones that run right along the crease of your finger. When it sliced in, I instantly felt the sting of it, so I threw the book down.

"The jokes are *that* bad?" Isaac asked. He's important—kind of the crux of this whole thing. He had this long brown hair that nearly touched his shoulders. I always told him to cut it, that he looked like a metal band reject that had been transported into modern times by some kind of horrible mistake. But now, I want nothing more than to run my fingers through that knotty, way-too-long hair.

"Paper cut," I said, pouting.

"Oh," he said with a laugh. "I'm sure you'll survive."

Heh.

I'll never know what was on that yellowed page that made my finger blow up to the size of a kielbasa. I just know how incredibly lame it is that a *paper cut* started the zombie apocalypse. I warned you, right? This story doesn't start like you'd expect. Hell, if I thought the world was going to end because of the undead, I'd think something like a lab experiment gone wrong or some disease that gets started by a necrophiliac fucking the wrong corpse or something. I don't know. Just not a paper cut from a book full of terrible jokes.

But shit happens.

I'm going to take a break. My hand is getting crampy.

***

So I went to the hospital. Isaac took me there, and he was feeling bad for making fun of me for pouting over the little cut, considering how my entire arm had gone red and my veins were clearly visible through my skin. They had darkened so much that they looked like thick, black webs shooting through my body. Looking in the mirror made me want to throw up.

When the doctors started to check me out, it was clear from their hushed discussion that they had no idea what the hell was going on with me. My lips were bloated to the point where I couldn't even formulate words, so Isaac told them about the paper cut. The doctors said that they hardly thought that was the cause of what was going on with me, but that they'd look into it. As they flashed lights in my eyes and examined my finger, my vision blinked out and, whether my eyes were closed or open, all I saw was red. The hushed voices became distant as I faded into what I thought must've been sleep.

When I woke up, I knew something was wrong. I sat up straight in bed, surrounded by this intense chatter,

3

and there were more doctors and nurses in the room than I'd ever even seen on *Grey's Anatomy*. It was *packed* in there, and they were all looking at me as if waiting for me to say something. I tried my mouth out, and found that I could move my lips again. In fact, everything felt normal. I said the first thing that came to mind.

"What's up, guys?"

And then, more chatter. I tried to catch a word here or there, but I was still woozy from being asleep. Finally, one of the doctors started to usher everyone out of the room, and I was left alone with the one that I remembered from before. The guy who said that he didn't think it had been a paper cut.

"My name is Doctor Franks. How are you feeling, Minnie?" he asked.

"Like I took a whole bunch of drugs," I said. "Which, I'm pretty sure I did, right? I feel like I slept for a week."

"Not a week," he said. "Three days."

"Three days?" I said. "What the hell did you guys give me, an elephant tranq?"

"And…" he took in a deep breath and looked from side to side. If I wasn't mistaken, he looked embarrassed of what he was about to say. "You weren't quite…asleep."

"Oh," I said. "Wow. So I was…I was in a coma?"

The doctor looked at me over his bifocals. "Minnie, you died forty times in the past three days."

I think if I saw something like this on TV (probably a soap opera), I would expect the girl to either faint or laugh it off or get this "OH MY GOD" look in her eyes before they cut to commercial. But I just…it's hard to really know what to *say* to something like that. So I reverted to what I usually do when my brain can't process something.

"I died forty times from a paper cut?" I said. "Wow, I'm a bit of a pussy."

Dirty jokes.

The doctor didn't laugh, though. He bowed his head and said, "Minnie, I wish we had more to tell you. Something was introduced into your system, likely because of the...ahem...paper cut, but we...we've never seen anything like it before. It's at once destructive and regenerative, which might be what...erm, killed you and brought you back to...I'm sorry, am I sounding ridiculous? I feel ridiculous. I've just never seen anything *like* this before."

"No worries, doc," I said, trying to ignore the fact that my heart was pumping twice the normal speed in my chest, and that I was beginning to get very, very scared. Keep on joking. Keep on joking. I had to just keep cracking the jokes, because my *next* reaction is to hole up and go catatonic (Note: that happens later—a lot). I said, "The extent of my medical knowledge is what I know from Doctors McDreamy and McSteamy, so you sound fine to me."

This time, the doctor allowed himself a brief smile. He told me that, despite my multiple *deaths* (how often do you hear that?), there seemed to be nothing wrong with me. I'd spent the last day just sleeping, seemingly one hundred percent healthy. He wanted to hold me there for tests for the rest of the week, which, of course, I agreed to. A girl dies, she figures it's best to do what the doctor says.

I was mad about missing work, because I loved goofing off, drinking coffee, and hanging out with my co-hosts. That kind of job keeps you sane, you know? But I stayed at the hospital for the week, even though I felt healthier than ever. Isaac visited me and, of course, he was a nervous wreck...so, of course, I made fun of him the whole time. But while I made joke after joke at his expense, he kissed me on the forehead and, even though I was in a hospital bed, wearing the least sexy gown-thing of all time, he made me feel beautiful.

Goddamn. I have to stop writing this before I get myself upset again.

***

Soon after that, I was back at work, joking around at the top of the building with my co-hosts Ray and Spinners. Ray, for those of you who don't listen to *What Up? It's the Morning*, is the funniest guy you'll ever meet. He's physically pretty frightening, with arms the size of my body and a stomach that could fit an entire classroom of first graders, but he is the archetypal friendly giant. Spinners, who started calling himself that when he bought a car with those rims that keep spinning after the car stops (yeah, I know, that's so 2002), is...well, if you're familiar with talk radio, you know that most comedy shows have a sleaze bag. Z100 has Skerry Jones, Hot97 has...well, *everyone*—you get the point. Spinners is our bag of sleaze, the guy who always says the wrong thing at the right time. On air, we love to hate him. Off air...well, kind of the same, but in a slightly more loving way.

I'm not ashamed to say that I fit another archetype in the show. I'm the *hot girl*. Every morning show has one. There is only one skill needed to be the hot girl: having "hot girl" voice. Truth is, the girl behind the voice could be the ugliest creature you've ever seen, but that's the charm of radio. You'll never *get* to see. Unless you search our names on the Internet (don't), but the way things seem to be going, I think the Internet might be gone by the time anyone reads this.

Anyway, the topic of the show when I returned? Obviously it was how much of a pussy I am because of my paper cut injury. I didn't tell Ray or Spinners that I'd died even once, much less forty times, because I had a hard enough time processing it myself. The only people that knew were the doctors, me, and Isaac, the last of whom had the distinct pleasure of mourning forty different times on each occasion the doctor told him that I was gone.

"So, I gotta say," Ray said, his deep oh-so-radio voice spilling out like honey. "I've never heard of someone going to the hospital for a paper cut."

"I'm never gonna hear the end of this, am I?" I asked.

"This begs the question," Spinners said, pausing for dramatic effect, before he added, "*Where* on your body did you get the cut?"

The both of us booed him, but Ray took it a step further and pressed the button that made a farting sound.

"What? I think that's a valid question!" Spinners said.

"You're not a valid person," I said.

"No, seriously," he said. "I just know that there are certain parts of the body that are more sensitive to—"

"Once Spinners starts talking about body parts, it's time to cut to break," Ray said. "We'll be back after these messages from..." He shuffled through a deck of cue cards, but came up with nothing. "...From those guys whose product you should buy. Those guys are the *best*."

"Oh, I love those guys," Spinners said.

"Who doesn't?" I added.

And then, Ray cut to break. Letting out a big rumble of a laugh, he patted me on the back and said, "Sorry for giving you hell. We're glad to have you back, really."

"Yeah, there's nothing worse than a room full of dudes," Spinners said.

"Thanks for your concern. How did you guys manage to do so many shows without killing each other?"

"Special guests," Ray said. "My brother came on."

"Wait, your brother?" I asked. "Your brother as in..."

Spinners nodded, twirling his finger next to his head.

"He isn't *crazy*," Ray said, smacking Spinners's hand away. "He's...eccentric. And eccentric makes for good radio."

"Exploiting your family," Spinners said. "I like it."

"Hey, if you have to exploit someone, it might as well be someone you love, right?" I said.

"He's doing better, anyway," Ray said.

"Every day, he told a different war story," Spinners said, snickering. "Dude has barely seen past his backyard, much less the Middle East."

"Be that as it may," Ray said, "he's also brilliant. He tells amazing stories, and you bet your ass he would be *awesome* in a war. He can make a bomb out of a freakin' bar of soap. What do you think happened to our in-ground pool? Shit went kaboom."

I was glad to be back at work with those guys. I missed them both. (Yes, even Spinners.) Unfortunately, that was the last time the three of us would ever host a show together. If it means anything, I think that our final show was pretty funny. If you listened, I hope you liked it. I hope it made your morning a bit better. That's all we ever wanted.

***

And then, I had another *last time I ever…*I went home to our cramped apartment and saw Isaac sitting at the computer, probably trying to sell some of his stuff on eBay. He's big on that. I wish I could say that the last night we spent together was the most romantic thing ever, that we somehow *knew* everything was about to change…but I just took a shower and he made me a sandwich and talked to me about this Jet Ski he wanted to buy. And then we watched a movie and went to bed and had nice sex and I slept a dreamless sleep.

When I write it all down now, it sounds like the most wonderful day of my life.

But then I woke up, and I knew something was wrong. My chin was covered in this black gunk, and I felt like hell. Isaac was already up, walking over to me with a wet towel.

"You were coughing all night," he said, pressing it into my chin, wiping the stuff away. I was terrified by how thick it looked on the towel.

"I was hacking up this shit all night and you're just now cleaning me?" I said, starting to freak out.

"No, that…that just happened. I already called the ambulance."

"You think I need it?"

"I don't know," he said. "But I want you to be safe. If you died *another* time, it would just be overkill."

"I see what you did there," I said, trying to calm myself down. "You should be a radio personality."

"I couldn't," he said, smiling at me. "I heard they're all ugly."

He held my hand until the ambulance came.

***

We got to the hospital, and Doctor Franks was already waiting to see me. Someone must've told him that the forty-times-dead girl was back. Things got really bright and freaky for a while as they examined me, but I found that, besides a bit of a sore throat, I felt completely fine. The doctors seemed to agree, as they could find absolutely nothing wrong with me.

After a few hours, I was once again alone in the room with Doctor Franks.

"So…you feel fine," he said.

"Besides the gross factor of coughing up tar, I'm not half bad."

"It's funny that you're here, Minnie, because—"

"Oh yeah," I cut him off. "I think this is a riot."

"I was going to say…because I was going to call you back here anyway," the doctor said. "To check up on how you're doing. I thought there might be a complication with…"

"Man, you sure can beat your way around a bush."

"As you know, I took blood samples from you," the doctor began.

Yeah, "as you know" is right. Ever since I was little, I've had a biiiiig issue with needles; doesn't matter if they're going in my arm, my teeth, anywhere. I don't do pointy.

"There was a slight issue with the samples," the doctor said.

"I'm going to guess that the blood did weird shit, but nothing seemed to be wrong with it," I said.

"Weird indeed."

"How weird?"

"The blood…again, I feel like a lunatic saying this, but it doesn't make it any less true—the blood combusted."

"Combusted meaning exploded?"

He nodded weakly.

"Ah," I said. "I guess I'm staying overnight for testing again, then?"

Another nod.

"Wow," I said. "Hey, you want to take any bets on how many times I'll croak?"

***

More testing. Of course, nothing conclusive. Nothing even a little bit intriguing, according to the doctor. I was starting to get used to that. Hell, I made a friend out of a nice old lady (Ethel…such an old lady name) who was sharing the room with me. She listened to me bitch about how Isaac hadn't even stopped by to visit me after my first day, and I listened to her stories about how her cats have serious issues relating to one another.

I was released without incident (incident meaning multiple deaths) a few days later. And that, I guess, is what you've all been waiting for. When shit begins to hit the fan.

I came home to a wrecked apartment. And I don't mean "Isaac forgot to put his underpants away" wrecked. I mean liquidation sale wrecked. I mean "let the kids play with whatever they want" wrecked. I mean "there's a zombie lumbering around in my apartment" wrecked. Particularly the latter, be-cause...well...

When I came in, about to give Isaac a piece of my mind for leaving me to hang out with an old lady for days on end, I saw it. The creature was hunched over, banging itself into my bookshelf. David Sedaris and Aus-tin Boroughs rained down on its head. I screamed (more of a battle cry, I like to think) and ducked to the floor, reaching under the bed where Isaac and I keep our bat in case an intruder...you know, intrudes. I grabbed the bat, gripped the handle, and reeled back, ready to go upside the creature's head.

But then it turned around.

I dropped the bat to the floor.

"Isaac?" I said.

He groaned in reply. His lips were coated in the same black substance that I'd coughed up just a few days earlier. I put my hand to my mouth to keep from scream-ing as my eyes traveled up his face, saw how his greyed skin hung so loosely from his bones that I could see moist, red flesh under his eyes. The long hair that I al-ways complained about had fallen from his scalp in clumps, which I saw were all over our floor. He reached out a hand to me. I gasped, taking a step back.

Isaac didn't react. He kept walking, staggering toward the door. He was wearing shorts, and I looked at his legs to see why he was walking like that. His normal-ly muscular calves were drooping down like flab, and I could see black veins through his nearly transparent skin just like when I was first infected.

"Isaac," I said, and this time it was a sob. He walked toward the open door, not reacting to his name. As he lumbered out of the house, all I could do was fall to the floor and cry, knowing only two things for sure. First, that this was so very much my fault. Whatever I was carrying had infected him when I'd coughed it up, only it hit him much worse. Two...I knew what he looked like. I felt ridiculous thinking it. As I mentioned before, everyone knows about zombies. Even people who don't watch horror films know what a zombie looks like, how they act...what they want to eat.

As soon as he disappeared from sight, his arms outstretched in front of him like such a stereotype, I couldn't process that I'd let a zombie out on the world. All I knew was that I'd killed the guy that I love. I curled into a ball and didn't get up for longer than I'm okay with admitting.

God, I need a break.

***

I spent a long time thinking about what to do next.

Thing is, I have a tendency to suck at taking action. I'm very much a "hole up until the bad situation" goes away kind of girl. The best example I can think of this is my friendship with Ruby. Ruby was my best friend in high school, but things got a bit tricky when she, on the day of our graduation, told me that she was in love with me. As you might have gathered from my having written about Isaac, I don't swing that way. I could have easily told Ruby that she might have misinterpreted our friendship but that I would like to keep hanging out. That's what I wanted to say. That's what the smart thing would have been. But I didn't. I just ran away and stopped answering her calls. I know, it was a disgusting thing to do, but I didn't mean it to be hurtful. I was just too afraid to do anything. I knew that anything I said would break her, so I hoped that if I said nothing, she would just think I was an asshole and move on. Ruby died in a fire the next year—I found out on Facebook of all places. I hated myself for not being with her that past year, and I wonder, even now, what she thought of me when she died. I wonder if she thought I was a terrible person.

I ended up writing a long e-mail to her, telling her how important she was to me, how I missed her, and how I was so, so sorry. Of course, the e-mail didn't matter and would stay unread forever…but it helped me a little bit, I guess. But again, I acted too late.

Clearly, I hadn't learned from my mistake, because I let my Isaac walk out of the house, sick like he was, and I didn't do anything until a day later. When I finally forced myself to get up, I called the police, but when they asked what exactly had happened and what I wanted them to do, I hung up. I was at a loss for words. How could I possibly tell them without seeming like I was pranking? And trust me, I know prank phone calls. I am the Prime Mistress of Prankery.

With nothing else to do, I did what I knew best. I drove to the radio station. Not that I thought it would help. I just knew that if I let myself soak in my own panic for much longer, I would completely lose it.

When I got there, Ray and Spinners were replaying a classic prank phone call that I'd done on this really skeezy mattress company. It was a pleasant distraction to walk into a room with two of my friends laughing at something that I'd done, but the happy feeling didn't last. My brain had been a complete mess since Isaac left, and it was hard enough to focus on what I wanted to ask these guys. They noticed me standing off to the side of the control board when the prank came to an end. Looking taken aback, Ray swerved his seat over to the microphone and said, "Something tells me that Minnie will be back soon, ladies and gents. Let's take a break…and remember. We love you in a way that makes us tingly in our pants."

They came over to me and asked how I was doing, why I hadn't called, and a whole bunch of other stuff that I couldn't process. I waited until they stopped asking me questions before I took a deep breath and, massaging my temples, said, "Have you noticed anything weird?"

They both looked at me as if I'd just taken a shit in the middle of the floor.

"Um…besides everything that's been going on with you?" Spinners asked.

"Give her a minute, man," Ray said, slapping Spinners on the shoulder. "Min, you'd get a kick out of this. I was waiting to tell you all day. Some lunatic on the news is saying that—"

"I think I did something terrible," I said. "I…"

I looked at my two co-hosts, the men who were admittedly my best friends in the world…and I spun around and ran away. What else could I do? Could I tell them that I think I made my boyfriend into a zombie? No. That doesn't happen in real life. That's not a problem that people like me have. All I'm supposed to worry about is if my jokes are still funny, if I'm starting to develop a muffin-top over my pants, and when the hell Isaac is going to propose to me. I'd been stupid to go to the radio station. I hadn't been thinking clear. It was obvious, really.

Leaving Ray and Spinners confused as all hell, I ran through the parking lot to get to my car. As I approached it, I saw that there was a man hunched over, clawing at the window as if trying to scratch through the glass.

"Hey!" I said, going into offense mode in an instant. I guess it's that New Yorker instinct. The man turned around and, for a moment, I froze—it was Isaac. But then when he took a shaky step toward me, holding a bloated hand out, I saw him clearly more clearly. Not Isaac. Not Isaac at all. There was a decidedly different…God, I still feel silly writing this, but there was a different goddamn zombie walking toward me, a moist gurgle bubbling up from the back of his throat.

As I may have mentioned before, I'm a fighter. If there's a guy in my house, I go for the bat. Someone tries to break into my car, I'm ready to fight. But for some reason, with this monster walking toward me, surely thinking that he'd like nothing better than to crack open my skull and eat the chewy center, I closed my eyes and did nothing. I just waited, paralyzed by the realization that whatever I'd done wasn't limited to Isaac. Of course it wasn't. I'd been so obsessed with the idea of the man I love being gone that I didn't even think about what he could spread.

The zombie's hot, putrid breath washed over my face, dampening my nose. I waited to feel the swollen hands grab at my face. I waited for the painful rip on my skull. But nothing happened. I opened my eyes and saw the creature staggering away.

Why didn't I feel relieved?

I got in the car and drove to the hospital, not wanting to give myself another second to process what that meant.

And that's how it all fell apart, I guess. Because I put stuff off. Because I don't think about fallout. Because I'm too scared to examine meaning. I didn't think about what would happen if Isaac left, and I didn't let myself ponder the infection issue long enough to make the connection between what had happened when I coughed up the black shit to the "combustion" of my blood at the hospital. Once I pulled up, though, and saw the place surrounded by police and the fire department, it wasn't hard to guess what was going on.

I parked across the street and scrambled out of the car. I was in front of a scene straight out of a horror movie.

They were all over. Zombies in scrubs, with stethoscopes, and in surgeon's masks, crawling on the grass as the police shot at them. Their faces were completely unrecognizable, but I knew that they had to be the people who worked on me. Doctor Franks was in there somewhere, but I would never be able to spot him from where I stood. Their faces were all droopy masks of flesh, just like Isaac's. There were other people standing where I had parked, taking in the scene with their hands to their mouths as if they were watching a house burn down. A grown man was on the floor, screaming. I followed his gaze and saw that it wasn't just the cops and the zombies in front of the hospital. There were patients running out of the back in different directions, sprinting across the lawn. Most of them were getting away, but the ones that the zombies got…

God, I don't even want to write it. I never even like to look at roadkill on the highways. I never thought I would see a person just get ripped open. But there it was, across the street from me. A lady, just some lady with brown hair. She tripped over her own feet, and one of the zombies grabbed her by the leg and dragged her across the grass. Bullets were flying through the monster's body, spraying black gunk everywhere, but it didn't stop. It dragged the woman into a cluster of the creatures, and they just completely tore her apart until there was nothing left but red and bone.

I remember wishing I could've thrown up. But I just stood there, my mouth hanging open, watching horrible death happen all because of me. I wondered if Isaac was off somewhere, ripping someone in half, too.

***

It's easy to joke around about what you'd do during a zombie apocalypse. Who you'd want on your survival team, what weapons you'd use, how many zombies you think you'd kill per week, etcetera, etcetera. But when it really happens, there's nothing left to do but to be afraid. This is another instance where I'm not proud of my actions, but what else could I have done? If anyone was going to stop this shit, it wasn't going to be me. What could I do? Nothing but go home, slide into bed, and listen to "I Want to Hold Your Hand" over and over again. It was *our* song. When we first started dating, Isaac made me this mixtape with just that song over and over. It was cheesy, yet so charming. I know you probably hate me by this point, because I'm acting like some lovesick fucking teenager while the world falls apart around me, but all I wanted to do was close my eyes and pretend that I was back in time on a happier day with a guy that loved me when my town wasn't being overrun with monsters from B-movies.

After a few days—I know, don't judge me—I turned on the news. I don't know what I expected to see, but my worst fears were realized when I flicked from station to station and got nothing but static on every channel. I tried the radio, but it didn't work. At that point, I was too scared to log onto the Internet to confirm the reason for all of this. I wondered if anyone knew it was my fault. I wondered how many people were dead because of a paper cut. How many people were just infected and completely hollowed out by a virus that, for some reason, made its home in my body. Those people would never hug anyone again. They would never laugh or dance or sing their favorite song to the person they love.

And that…that is when I got the idea that led me back to the radio station, where I am now; writing this entirely too long confession. My hand is cramped to shit. I need to take one last break.

***

You all know what I saw when I left my house. It's what you've been living. The dead seemed to outnumber the living, and the destruction was as far as you could see. People were being chased down and eaten, or torn apart like that poor woman in front of the hospital…but not me. For some reason, I was able to walk to my car in the apartment parking lot, right past a group of zombies feasting on a dog that was still whimpering. One of them looked at me, cocking his head to the side as if in recognition, but none of them made a move to jump me. Maybe I smelled like one of them. Maybe they knew I was the one they came from. I don't know, and frankly I don't care about the sci-fi bullshit behind it. It did, however, make my drive to the radio station easier. I brought my bat with me though, just in case.

The closer I got, however, the more zombies there were. When I was just a block away, I had to get out of my car and push through a crowd of the undead as if I were at a Walmart on Black Friday. Something was making them flock to the radio station, but I had no idea what it was. As I squeezed through, I saw a big van parked in front of the building. It was the only car I'd seen besides mine that wasn't turned over on the side or run off the road. The closer I got, however, I saw that this van was even worse off than the other. Zombies were clawing their way in through the broken windows, and spurts of blood smacked against the windshield. Whoever was in there was not doing well. I didn't recognize the vehicle, and I had no idea who would've attempted to get into the station besides me.

I finally made my way into the door of the building. I made use of the bat, knocking zombies away from the staircase entryway as I went inside. They might not have been after me, but I didn't want them in control room when I did what I planned on doing. I needed to be alone.

There were a few that had somehow made it into the stairwell, and I batted them away with swift strikes to the head. I *might* have had a passing thought that I was right about how badass I would be in the event of the zombie apocalypse, but I was too focused to really appreciate it. For once, right? And anyway, when you've got nothing left to care about, jokes don't really seem to have the same effect.

I've learned that from writing this.

I got to the top floor, but found that the door to the control room was locked. Peering into the glass window, I was astonished to see Ray at the panel, tweaking a knob. Thrilled to see a friend, I banged on the door, and watched as he jumped so high that he fell off of his chair. When he got up, though, he came with a friggin' shotgun, so I threw my hands up in the air, waving in the least zombie-like fashion I could. He squinted, slowly lowering the gun.

A moment later, I was in the room with him, staring out the window at a horde of hundreds, maybe thousands of zombies. I had so many questions for him, and I'm sure he had a lot for me. I wanted to ask if he knew what had happened to Spinners. If he knew who the person in the van was. But I put those questions off. I was just happy to be standing next to him.

"The zombies…I brought 'em here," he said quietly. He was looking out the window, but his gaze was blank.

"Why?" I asked.

He shrugged. "Got nothing left. Figured me and my brother would blow 'em up. I told you he's good with making things go *boom*." With a laugh, he added, "Spinners was right, by the way. I guess he is a bit crazy. I don't know how my brother knows half the shit he does. He told me that if I broadcasted a goddamn dog whistle over the big speakers…you know, the ones that we use for the public shows?"

"Yeah," I said. Those speakers were loud enough for the whole town to hear. They were the very reason I'd driven there.

"Well, we recorded a dog whistle and played it. He told me they would come. And they did. And now, the two of us are gonna take these fuckers out. Together. I think my brother is *excited* to be in the thick of this. It's like one of his made-up stories come true."

"Your brother…" I said. "Where is he?"

"Getting stuff ready in the van," he said. "Somewhere down there. He thinks the explosion will be big enough to take the whole building down. Crush the zombies that it doesn't blow up. Heh. Hell, maybe it'll be enough to help. I figure it's a noble death, right? Spinners would be proud."

"Ray," I said gently. "I saw the van, and he…you know."

Ray looked at me. I expected him to cry, to deny it, to do something. But he just looked at me and then, after a long moment, he let out one bitter chuckle. "Oh. Well, there goes that idea."

The two of us stood in silence, the only living things within miles.

"Why are you here?" he asked.

"I, uh…"

I didn't want to tell him. I feel weird even writing it. I just sat down at the control panel and pulled a CD out of my pack. I looked at the freshly burned disc and said, "I just wanted to play a song."

I don't think Ray was listening anymore though. He was already walking out of the room as he said, "I'm gonna go take a leak." I love Ray, but when I'd taken the CD out, it was as if he'd already gone. I was holding my final hope.

I switched the big speakers over to the CD system. I put the CD in and hit play. And then…sweet music.

"I Want to Hold Your Hand" began pumping out over the big speakers, playing for the entire town—whoever was left, that is. I looked down at the zombies, searching for Isaac. That's all I wanted in the end. I wanted to see if there was anything left, if he would come to me, if he would stand on top of the van and recognize the lyrics and come back to me. If I could just see one moment of pause in *any* of them, it would be enough for me to go on.

I watched, waiting, searching the endless crowd for any sign of recognition in the monsters.

I never really thought it would work. It was just a stupid hope.

I stared at the army of undead, begging for one of them to stop thrashing around and just listen to the goddamn song. I scanned every area, looked at each and every one of them, but nothing. I hit play again and looked again, and then again and again.

Nothing.

There was nothing left.

Of course there was nothing left.

***

I found Ray dead in the bathroom a couple of minutes ago. He put the gun in his mouth and...I don't want to write what I saw.

I looked at the body of my friend, another person dead because of me, and I realized that I didn't have much of a choice but to follow. I know that sounds all "woe is me," but I don't think I *should* be alive. I'm carrying this thing. It's *in* me. And plus, what the hell is there to live for anyway? Everything is gone. Everything is dead.

One of my favorite staples of zombie fiction is when the good guys cover their bodies or cars in zombie guts so they could safely walk past the undead. Those scenes are so tense, so gross, and so clever. I'm different, though. I have that stuff on the inside. I can walk safely to the van, find whatever explosives Ray and his brother were getting together, and blow the fuck out of this place, taking out an entire town's worth of undead with me. It's the least I can do, right? I don't know much about explosives, but with all of these zombies gathered here... it would have to put a big dent in their numbers. It'll at least take the building down, apparently. I hope the explosion doesn't get to these papers, though, because I think it's important for people to know what happened. Maybe not important for mankind, because a paper cut isn't really something you can avoid or learn from...but it's important to me. I want people to know how sorry I am.

So I guess this is it. If this whole apocalypse thing ever blows over, maybe people will eventually find this and know that I caused it. Me. Just some crazy lady who told dumb jokes on the radio at the asscrack of dawn. It's funny, though. As I'm writing this, knowing that everything has crashed down around me and I have absolutely nothing left, I can't help but think about when my friend Ruby died. Writing her that e-mail made me feel better, sort of, so I hoped this would do the same. Hell, I really

21

don't want to spend my last ten minutes alive thinking about how much I suck.

I don't want this to make you hate me more than you already do—if there even *is* a "you" around to be reading this—but I can't even think big picture right now. As I write this, I'm looking out the window at an endless army of the undead, and all I can think about is how I killed my boyfriend. I miss him and I love him and I want him to put his forehead on mine. When he would do that, his hair would hang between the two of us like curtains so that no one could see when he gave me a private little kiss. That will never happen again.

I'm sorry for a lot of things. I'm sorry that I picked up that stupid little book, I'm sorry that I didn't demand to stay in the hospital until they knew what was going on, and I'm sorry that shit turned out the way it did. But I hope the fact that I wrote this means something. I don't want folks to think this was some chemical accident or something that the government did or some cooky shit like that. I need people to know how *silly* this whole thing was.

I'm going down in history as the girl that ended the world...but hey, I hope a few people out there remember listening to my morning show. I hope they remember my prank phone calls, stupid jokes, and how I never gave Spinners a break. I hope you remember the good stuff. I hope I made you laugh on the way to work in the morning. I hope I made you, if only for a moment, smile.

The Zombie Curse

By Bennie L. Newsome

96:00 hrs

Justin Burrows awoke with a start.

Oh no, the man thought as he threw the stifling comforter aside. He quickly rolled over to retrieve his cellphone from the floor. The bed, which had apparently seen too much action, groaned loudly beneath his weight. The man reached into his pants pocket and removed his mobile device. He slid the phone open and a bright illumination appeared.

"Shit!" Justin exclaimed when he saw that there were six missed calls and the time read 2:13 in the morning.

He jumped out of bed, causing the woman who was still wrapped in the comforter to roll onto her side. "Hey, Clari…uh, Meris…Tiffa…hey, girl, can I take a shower real quick."

The woman moaned and lazily waved her hand.

"Thanks."

He caught a glimpse of her bare thigh before he hurried to the bathroom. The sight brought back memories of flashing lights, loud music, and lots of alcoholic beverages. He remembered seeing "whatever her name was" out on the dance floor. It was her thighs that caught his attention, but the way she gyrated her hips made him approach her. Justin had a strong desire to know if she was just as talented horizontally as she was vertically.

A smile found its way onto his face when he thought about their romp in the sheets. She had been better than her advertisement had foretold, and he got to sample her in every way possible.

***

23

Justin clicked the bathroom light on and hurried over to the tub. The small room resonated with the sound of his feet slapping against the linoleum floor. Like his naked feet, there was not a stitch of clothing on the rest of his body. He seldom wore clothes unless it was mandatory. The man was proud of his body, to the point of vanity.

Justin Burrows was tall, dark, and handsome. His low cut hair was glossy black and wavy, because of all the attention he gave to his head. The man's hair—both on his head and face—was neatly trimmed from visiting the barbershop on a weekly basis. His skin tone was that of light chocolate, and his physique showed that he went to the gym regularly. Justin had no shortage of female attention and he never hesitated when it came to satisfying his lustful desires.

Squeak...squeak...squeak. The bathtub handle screeched as Justin first turned on the hot water, then the cold. When the water temperature was right, he turned the knob in the center and the shower spewed warm water. Justin hadn't planned on staying so late, but sleep overcame him and he was powerless to stop it. "No name" in there had really put his endurance to the test.

Justin found himself smiling again.

94:52 hrs

An hour and eight minutes later, Justin brought his gold Nissan Pathfinder to a slow creep as he entered the driveway of a beautiful, single story house; the very same house that he shared with his wife, Talisha Burrows. As a precautionary measure, the radio was silent and the headlights had been turned off a couple of blocks back. The man's thumping heart was the only sound that could be heard in the vehicle.

Eeeeek...eeek...eeeeeeeeeeeek! Justin gritted his teeth as his squealing brakes shattered the night's silence. His hopes of sneaking into the house might have just been thwarted, because he was too much of a procrastinator to go and get his brakes inspected. *I'll do it this weekend,* Justin promised himself. It was the very same oath he made every time he tried to sneak home unnoticed.

When he brought the car to a halt, the man placed the gear in park and killed the engine. He stared through his dusty windshield and looked at his home. There were no lights on anywhere in the house and he didn't see the glow from a television. No signs of life.

Looks are deceiving, he told himself. *She'll be waiting up for me. I'm one hundred percent sure of it.*

Justin slowly opened the door and gingerly stepped out. He pushed the door close as softly as possible. The door was not fully shut, but it would have to suffice until morning. He took a deep breath before tiptoeing across the driveway and up the concrete path. Justin came to a stop in front of the mahogany door. As he readied his keys, the door swung open unexpectedly.

"AHHHHHH!" Justin screamed after being startled by the sudden movement.

"Uh huh! I caught your stupid ass!" his wife, Talisha said. She crossed her small arms in front of her bosom. "You need to get your damn brakes fixed!"

"I'll make sure to get them fixed this week," he said as he forced his way into the house.

Talisha slammed the door close and locked it before storming after her husband. "So what's your excuse for coming in at three o'clock in the morning? Huh? What trick you been screwing that would keep you out so late? Musta been good!"

"Ain't nobody screwing no tricks, man! Every time I come home late, you always gotta assume I was out with some female. Why I couldn't been hanging with my boys?"

"You wasn't with your boys!" Talisha yelled as she followed Justin through the living room and down the hallway to their bedroom. "I called Pookie and he said he ain't seen you all night!"

Justin came to a sudden halt and turned around to face his wife. "First of all, you don't need to be having Pookie's number, and you ain't got no business calling him—"

"I didn't call Pookie's cellphone cause I *ain't* got the number. I called Monique…and Pookie happened to be at home when he was suppose to be!"

"Well…" Justin said as he turned around and continued to make his way to the bedroom. "I wasn't with Pookie n'dem. I was with some other friends."

"You ain't got no other friends!"

Justin started stripping down to his underclothes. "You don't know all of my friends! I happened to be hanging out with some guys from work."

"Okay, so where y'all been?" Talisha wanted to know.

"We was at the club!"

"Until three in the morning?"

"We left the club around two something, I got home at three."

"Why you ain't answer the phone when I was calling you?"

"In the club?" Justin asked as if that was the craziest thing he had ever heard. "You got the music going and all the people talking, nobody ain't hearin' no phone!"

"You were at the club 'til two in the morning?" Talisha asked.

"That's what I said," Justin replied.

Talisha leaned forward and sniffed her husband. "You expect me to believe that you've been at the club all night and you smell like Irish Spring soap? You must think I'm some kind of fool! What man goes to the club all night around all that drinking and smoking and dancing and come home smelling like he just hopped out the shower?"

Justin didn't have an answer for that one. What could he say? That he was posted up against the wall all night away from everybody? With no other alternatives, the man decided to follow the cheater's protocol for instances of being caught in a lie. Transfer blame.

"Man, I ain't got time for this," he mumbled as he headed out of the room.

"And where you going?" Talisha asked.

Justin spun around angrily and shouted, "I'm going to the couch! Is that okay with you? Because I ain't come home to be given the third degree about where I been and who I've been with. You asked me and I told you. I was with some guys from work and we went to the club. I ain't got no reason to lie. What you need to do is work on your insecurities, because I love you and I've never been unfaithful, but you don't want to hear that! Naw, you want to hear that I was out screwing some other female! If that's what you want to hear, then yeah, I was out screwing some female until three in the morning."

Justin turned away and headed down the hallway. "Ain't that much sex in the world!" he mumbled loud enough for Talisha to hear him. The man had lied so well that he had actually convinced himself that *he* had been wronged. He was truly upset!

"But you gonna believe what you wanna believe!"

Talisha just stood in the bedroom doorway, too shocked to say anything else. Crisis averted.

91:50 hrs

As the morning continued to progress and sunlight began to peek over the horizon, Justin tossed and turned on the living room couch, dreaming of the woman with no name.

She sat straddled atop him with her entire glory unveiled. His big, strong hands grasped her rocking hips. Justin's lustful eyes roved up her flat, caramel-colored stomach and paused on her firm, bouncing breasts. After several moments, his sights continued to travel upward along her slender neck and settled on her face. The woman's visage was twisted into an expression of ecstasy.

No name's moans mingled with Justin's grunts of pleasure. Their harmonizing was added to the smacking sound of their flesh and the creaking of the worn out bed. The headboard thumped against the wall, completing the beautiful instrumental entitled Love Making.

Justin laid his head back onto the pillow and closed his eyes. He found delight in the wonderful music they made together. He relished the sensation that he felt between his legs.

All of a sudden, the woman's groans became indecipherable words.

I got her speaking in tongues, *Justin thought proudly.*

He opened his eyes to see her face. The man's smile was instantly wiped from his countenance and replaced with a look of horror. The woman was gone, and in her stead was a red, demonic creature. Long, spiral horns protruded from the sides of her head. Her pupil-less eyes were fiery red and filled with menace and loathing. The demon's face was grotesque, but its body was still that of the nameless woman.

A part of Justin screamed that he should knock the demon off of him and run as fast as he could, but there was another part—the piece between his legs—that insisted there was nothing wrong. If a feeling that good was wicked, then he didn't want to be right. Justin had always thought with his smaller head, and he did not see why he should stop at that point. The man closed his eyes and enjoyed the ride.

Eventually, the demon's tempo sped up. Their flesh collided more frequently, more aggressively. The bed sounded like it was going to hit the floor at any minute and the headboard threatened to knock a hole in the drywall. The moans and grunts became screams of unbearable pleasure.

Justin dug his fingers into the demon's hips, the beast clawed his chest. The pair reached their climatic points simultaneously, and then the sexual activity came to a sudden halt. So did the dream.

Without warning, Justin suddenly sat upright. His breaths were labored; sweat came down his face in rivulets. The man wiped a hand across the top of his head as he scanned the room. After making sure he was in his living room, he breathed a sigh of relief.

What the hell was that about, Justin wondered.

91:22 hrs

A few minutes later, Justin turned off the shower and stepped out of the tub. With his bizarre dream forgotten for the moment, he found himself to be in a good mood. The day was new, he smelled good, he looked good, and he was feeling good. He couldn't ask for more.

Justin snatched his towel off the metal rack and made his way across the steamy room while whistling a catchy tune. He quickly dried off then tossed the heavy cloth down, giving him something to stand on other than the moist floor. Justin's whistling turned into a hum as he grabbed his toothbrush, applied toothpaste to the bristles, and began brushing his teeth.

All the while, the mirror was clearing up.

In the middle of brushing his teeth, Justin happened to look at himself in the mirror. The humming ceased along with the teeth cleaning. He spit the toothpaste into the sink and quickly returned his sights to his reflection.

"What the hell!" Justin whispered as he ran a hand across his bare chest. The dream crossed his mind momentarily. Eight, long whip marks ran from his pectorals down to his abdominal region. Marks were no good when they didn't come from his wife.

"That broad scratched the shit out of me!"

Justin quickly rinsed his mouth out. Afterwards, he walked over to the spot where his recently shed clothing lay on the floor. He picked up his undershirt from the pile and hurriedly put it on. Talisha would kill him if she happened to see those scratches. Speak of the Devil...

The bathroom door opened and Talisha entered wearing a pink bra and panty set. Strutting around in her underwear was the woman's subtle way of saying, "I'm sorry."

"Hey...hey, baby...what's up? What you want?" Justin stood in the middle of the room with nothing on but a musty undershirt.

"Justin, I just wanted to apologize for the way I overreacted last night. You know I can get very jealous and...it gets out of hand sometimes. I know you love me and I know you would never do anything to hurt me."

Justin smiled awkwardly and held out his arms. "Come here, baby."

Talisha returned the smile as she walked over to him and became embraced within his big, strong arms. "I don't mind when you get jealous, but you gotta trust me when I tell you stuff. This marriage can't last without trust."

She pulled back a bit so she could look into his big, brown eyes. "I know, baby."

Justin leaned down and kissed Talisha. When he pulled away, she stood on tiptoes to return the tender gesture. Before long, their quick smooches turned into passionate kisses. Justin picked Talisha up and sat her on the edge of the bathroom sink. At the moment, he was wondering why he would even cheat on a good woman like her. Talisha was everything he desired in a spouse.

The woman was slim and had vivacious curves in all the right places. She was light-skinned, and had long, luxurious black hair. Justin's heart would always speed up when he looked into her gorgeous, hazel eyes. The man loved the freckles that dotted her nose. Besides looks, Talisha had a great personality and a good job.

Justin came to the realization that greed caused him to risk everything on brief encounters with women that meant nothing to him. Although he was aware of the fact that his gluttonous appetite for the opposite sex could possibly ruin his marriage, the man had no intentions of changing his sinful ways. He would end his adulterous habits one day, but that day was not coming anytime soon.

Talisha took her small hands and began to go under his shirt, seeking the rigidness of his muscles. An alarm went off in Justin's head. He quickly grabbed her hands and placed them around his neck. She giggled and he smiled back. When they resumed kissing, Justin's hands traveled down her sides, along her legs, between her thighs, and finally came to explore her most sacred spot. With one hand, he moved her panties aside.

Justin felt that she was ready, he was born ready. He took a step forward and Talisha gasped as he entered her.

The bathroom began to fog up again, but this time it was not because of hot water. Talisha wrapped her hands around his waist as they continued their dance. Justin gripped her legs and lifted them higher into the air. Their lips parted from one another's in order to make way for the moans that had built up within them. Justin gently kissed the side of his wife's face. After her face, he showered her neck with passionate kisses and then moved down to her collarbone.

"OUCH!" Talisha shouted suddenly. She automatically hit Justin in his arm and pushed him away. "You bit me!"

"I…I'm sorry, baby…I don't know—"

Talisha looked at her shoulder. Pinpoints of blood had begun to rise from his teethmarks. She jumped down from the sink and fixed Justin with an angry and bewildered stare. "I guess that's what that trick you sleeping with likes, huh? She likes it rough?"

Justin reached out for her. "Baby I—"

"Don't touch me!" Talisha screamed as she dodged his hand and ran from the bathroom.

Justin could do nothing but watch her leave. He wanted to chase her. His entire being demanded that he run after her, but how could he explain the fact that he had just bitten her shoulder. He looked into the mirror and stared at his puzzled reflection.

"What the hell is going on with me?"

86:17 hrs

It was a beautiful day in Birmingham, Alabama. The sun continued its ascent into the dazzling blue sky, paused for an hour to admire its domain, then began its slow descent. Fluffy white clouds drifted sluggishly across the blue backdrop, going out of their way to avoid hindering the sun's rays. Despite the splendor of it all, things for Justin went from good to bad to worst.

The man struggled to make it through the nine hour work day. By his second hour at work, Justin could barely walk a couple of steps without collapsing into a chair. Once lunch time came around, he was experiencing a terrible migraine and his strength was steadily waning.

The ill man sat at a long, fold-out table in the break room, staring at his microwave lunch. Since asking Talisha to make him something to eat was out of the question, he had to grab the first thing he saw in the freezer. Before him sat one of the healthy meals his wife was always buying when she went on one of her dieting kicks, but she never seemed to eat them. Justin could see why.

The aroma wafting up from the black, plastic tray made him nauseous. He wasn't sure if the cause was the horrible smell, or his growing illness. Justin pushed the unappetizing food away and laid his throbbing head on the table and closed his eyes.

Shortly after, the break room's double doors swung open and three individuals stepped into the room, laughing and talking. One of the guys spotted Justin and he walked over to the hurting man. "Hey, boss man! Saw you leaving the club last night with that fine redbone. Wish I could pull 'em like you do."

Metal screeched against concrete as the man pulled up a chair. The guy sat down and stared at Justin's bowed head. "Hey, boss man, are you alright?" the guy asked.

It took everything Justin had in him to lift his head. He started to open his eyes, but the act caused his skull to hurt worse, so he closed them again.

"Hey, Justin! Man you don't look so good!"

85:02 hrs

After his concerned co-worker went and talked to their supervisor, Justin was sent home early. A drive that normally took him fifteen minutes to complete turned into an hour and fifteen minute ride from hell. His migraine made it hard for him to focus on the traffic, so he had to drive extremely slow. After being honked at, cursed at, and rudely cut off several times, Justin decided to abandon the highway and take the back roads to his house. It turned out that the secondary route was just as terrible as the main route.

At one point, an old man pulled up alongside him on a two lane street, rolled down his window and yelled, "Get the fuck off the road!"

Justin was too drained to reply. All he could do was watch as the old man drove in front of him, cutting it dangerously close and peeled off. Justin stared at the old man's handicapped tag until it disappeared from sight.

Only by the grace of God, was Justin able to make it home safely and stumble through his front entryway. He shut the door quietly and locked it before slowly making his way to the bathroom. *I'm going to take a shower real quick then get some rest,* Justin thought. *I didn't get enough sleep last night. That has to be what's wrong with me.*

It took long enough, but Justin finally made it to the bathroom and began taking his clothes off. It proved to be an arduous task. Once the chore was complete, he situated the shower's water until the temperature was just right, then he carefully stepped into the tub. The steady flow of water spurting from the showerhead crashed against the bottom of the tub, creating a soothing sound like that of rain. Justin grabbed his bath rag and lathered it with soap.

Following the same procedure he had for twenty-eight years, Justin first washed his neck, his shoulders, and moved to his chest. After soaping up his chiseled chest, he washed his hairy arms, went down to his equally hairy legs, his feet, then came back up to wash his private area. As he covered his genitals in soap suds, the sexual organs fell off and hit the wet porcelain. SMACK!

Time froze.

The man moved as if he was in slow motion. Justin stared down at his genitals with an expression of astonishment on his face. His jaw dropped as he gawked at his most precious possession. The startled man looked between his legs, nothing there. Blood was not even present. His stuff had just…fallen off somehow. He returned his gaze back to the bottom of the tub. There it was, the whole set—both the faucet and the two knobs.

Time started ticking again.

Justin took a quick, deep breath and let loose a blood-curdling scream. "AHHHHHHHHHHH! AHHHHHHHHHH!" He no longer felt the skull splitting headache. His lack of strength had no effect on him at that moment. Justin jumped out of the tub, slipped on the wet floor and fell with a sickening thud. "Lord, no!" the man yelled as he bounced back up like a rubber ball and ran out of the bathroom. "This can't be happening to me! This can't be happening!"

Down the carpeted hallway he went, through the living room, and he came to a sliding skid in the kitchen. THUD! The wet, naked man fell again. Justin scrambled back up to his feet and frantically raided the kitchen cabinets. Pots and pans were thrown to the kitchen floor. Metal clanged against metal until he found what he was looking for—some Tupperware with a lid. Justin hurried over to the freezer, snatched the small door open and filled the container with cubes of ice. After all that was done, he ran back into the bathroom, picked his genitals out of the bathtub and stuffed it into the Tupperware.

A panicked Justin Burrows brought the transparent container up to his face. He stared at his penis and testicles, barely able to believe what he was seeing.

"AAAAAAAHHHHHHHHHHHHHHHHHHH!"

82:52 hrs

Justin pulled his mobile device from his pocket and looked at the time. The man let out a frustrated sigh. It had been over two hours since he first arrived in the emergency room of Mercy Hospital. He'd heard of doctors reattaching severed thumbs and such, but he had no clue if they could sew a set of genitals back on. And if they could, was there a deadline before the process was no longer applicable?

Come on people! What's taking so long, he wondered as he looked around the crowded lobby.

Every chair in the cramped room was full. Many people were forced to stand. Justin watched as individuals got up from their chairs to go to the vending machines, or visit the restroom only to return and find their stuff on the floor and their seats gone. Justin whimpered slightly as he thought about not having to worry with going to the restroom.

His Tupperware container was extremely cold against his flesh, but he refused to remove it from beneath his shirt. Justin did not want everybody looking at what was in the plastic box and they would most definitely look. They were nosey, all of them.

The man glared at the individuals in the room. He hated the fact that he had to be in there with those…those common folk. They were ugly, dirty, and full of germs. The uncouth people were conversing on ignorant topics, some of them coughed or sneezed without covering their mouths, and there was a snaggletoothed woman that kept staring at him with lecherous eyes.

Justin's right leg twitched rapidly as he glanced over at the window where the receptionist sat. The hospital employees were worse than the patrons. He had already been over there to take care of his paperwork, and it didn't take long for him to discover that they were not professional. He told the woman that he had a real emergency unlike the other wolf-criers in the waiting room, but she would not listen to him. Not only did she ignore him, but the woman was unnecessarily rude, and so was the old, crippled security guard. Justin thought about going into detail about his condition, but he refrained. They would most likely talk about him and laugh at his circumstance instead of aiding him.

If I wasn't carrying my dick in a box under my shirt, I would've caused a scene, Justin thought. *But the last thing I need right now is to call attention to myself.*

Without warning, one of the doors to the waiting room opened and a nurse stood in the doorway. She looked down at her chart and called, "Justin Burrows."

It's about time, Justin thought as he hurried over to the woman.

The impatient man was led into a back room and taken to a small table. The nurse asked him to have a seat as she walked around to the other side of the table and sat in her chair. The unconcerned woman began by asking him routine questions and Justin answered them while waiting on an opportune moment to explain his condition. It did not take long for him to find his opening.

"On a scale from one to ten," the woman began, "how would you rate your current level of pain?"

Justin gave the woman a smug look as he reached under his shirt and pulled out the Tupperware container. The sound of shifting ice could be heard as he sat the box on the table and removed the lid.

The nurse leaned over to look at the contents within. "Oh shit!" the woman exclaimed before covering her mouth with her hands.

Justin looked the woman in her startled eyes and asked, "How would you rate that?"

64:21 hrs

Things really sped up for Justin after that. Slam your penis on a table for the nurse to see and you automatically gain people's attention. Justin was quickly ushered into a small room that only had three walls and a curtain for privacy. A long, counter with a sink sat on one wall. Besides the counter covered in medical instruments, there was a mobile bed and a chair. Justin happened to be lying on the bed, staring up at the ceiling.

In no time at all, a doctor came by to have an initial look. The aged man was caught off guard by the plastic container that contained a set of genitals on a bed of ice. He was even more baffled by what he saw after checking Justin below the waist.

"I'm...I'm sorry, Mr. Burrows," the doctor said. He was dumbfounded to say the least. "I...uh...well, we can't sew that back on. Even if we could, which we can't, yours seemed to have…honestly, it looks like the flesh along your pelvis is decayed…rotten…causing your genitals to fall completely off. I've never seen anything quite like it."

Justin—that big, strong womanizer—burst into tears before the doctor could finish pronouncing his verdict. Sounding like a wounded wolf, Justin's wails brought onlookers down his hall. He could feel their stares and hear their whispers, but he didn't care. Their opinions did not matter; it was him who would have to go through life without an operating penis.

"Oh, Lord!" the blubbering man screamed at the ceiling. "Take me now, Lord! Send a big-ass bolt from the heavens and put a quick end to my now miserable existence!"

(Remove a man's family jewels and he instantly becomes a Shakespearian actor.)

"I'm truly sorry about your…about your loss," the doctor said over Justin's thunderous sobbing. "Um, I recommend that you stay here for a few days so we can run some test and see what caused…this."

"It's because I've been fooling around on my wife! I know it is! I sold my dick to the Devil and he came to collect! Aw, why me?"

"Very good. Uh…I'm going to take a few blood samples." The doctor filled two vials with Justin's blood then disappeared through the curtains, eager to be away from the shouting maniac.

In time, the man did stop weeping. It was then that Justin realized he could feel his headache and it was worst than it had been before. Not only was his migraine back, but he was no longer running on adrenaline so the man didn't have the strength to sit up any longer. Justin laid down on the paper covered bed and closed his teary eyes. Shortly after, the doctor returned with two other people dressed in white lab coats.

"These two are student doctors," the original doctor said. "I brought them here so they could observe your condition."

Justin didn't care.

"Hi, my name is Rebecca," the female student said. "This here is Robert."

The second student waved.

Justin simply replied with a limp wave of his own.

The female student proceeded by asking him a hundred questions while all three doctors took notes on their clipboards. Justin was asked to stand, bend, hold out his arms, and pose in many other positions. Although his head hurt terribly and he could barely stand, the broken man managed to follow orders while they poked at him and observed him.

Eventually, he was wheeled up stairs on a bed and dropped off in a room on the seventh floor. Throughout the night, Patient Care Technicians (PCTs) would come to him every couple of hours and stick him with needles and notate his blood pressure. He slept through majority of the visits. When he was awake, he was too disoriented to know who was who.

When morning came, six individuals came to his bed and looked him over. All wore white lab coats. They seemed pleasant enough, but Justin couldn't help feeling like an experiment. The head doctor talked about Justin as if he was a subject in a textbook and the other men and women took more notes.

After the doctors said their goodbyes, Justin was left alone for a minute then another PCT showed up with breakfast. Justin looked at the food; however, he had no desire for bacon, grits, eggs, and toast. He looked over at the homely looking woman as she took his blood pressure. The ill man could not stop from smacking his lips hungrily.

Justin stared at the rise and fall of the woman's breasts. *Two giant breasts with a side of warm liver,* the man thought. His eyes journeyed downward and he gazed at the woman's side. *Make that two giant breasts, a side of liver, and several large fat rolls. What the hell am I saying? Thinking of her as a to-go plate ...it's downright sadistic and well, cannibalistic.* He tried to alter his train of thought, and he did for a few seconds, but there was no way to halt the ravenous hunger that overcame him when he looked at the heavyset lady. He wanted her body.

The woman happened to catch him looking and she became very uncomfortable. There was something about Justin's eyes that sent a chill down her spine. She quickly removed the instrument from around his arm and hurried out of the room.

Justin let out a tiresome sigh, then turned over and went to sleep.

The man awoke some time later when another PCT entered the room. "Mr. Burrows, if you don't eat we're going to have to hook you up to an IV," the new arrival said.

"I'm just not..." Justin looked at the woman's succulent neck, "...hungry."

"Well, we'll take care of that. But right now you have a visitor."

Talisha, Justin quickly surmised. *I forgot all about her!*
"Send her in!"

The PCT left and another woman entered soon after. Justin glanced up and instead of looking into his wife's hazel eyes, he found himself gaping at the woman with no name. The lady was dressed in a red pants suit and a matching purse dangled from her arm on a gold chain. The man instantly thought of the red demon from his dream.

"How you doing, handsome?" she asked with a sinister smile.

64:20 hrs

"It's you!" Justin exclaimed in a weak voice. "You did this to me! You gave me AIDS?"

The woman laughed as she sat down in a brown, armchair near his bed. "AIDS? You wish you only had AIDS. No, sir, with AIDS you would have a sliver of hope. The STD you have now is a lot more deadly and fast acting."

Tears began to run down the side of Justin's face when he thought about his shriveled penis that was probably being dissected in a laboratory somewhere. "Why would you do this to me? I've never met you before last night. I've never done anything to you."

"I didn't choose you, sweetheart, *you* chose me," the woman said. "*You* saw me out there on that dance floor and *you*

39

just had to approach me instead of going home to your wife. *You asked if there was someplace we could go. You can't transfer the blame this time, Justin Burrows.* I gave you exactly what you wanted, which was the time of your life, and I got exactly what I wanted: an excellent subject for my zombie curse."

"Zombie curse?"

"Ah, yes! The zombie curse. Are you familiar with the seven deadly sins, Mr. Burrows?"

With a nod of his head, Justin indicated that he did know about the seven deadly sins.

The woman gave him a wicked smile. "Well, a perfect subject for the zombie curse has to have all seven qualities. He's got to be angry, greedy, a procrastinator, prideful or vain, full of lust, envious, and gluttonous. To be honest, those qualities can be found in just about every soul on Earth, but only those with large quantities of each would be pulled toward me."

Justin thought about how the seven deadly sins related to him. "You said that I would have to possess all seven sins, but there's one missing. Envy. I've never been envious of anyone."

"That's not true. Remember two weeks ago, how you slept with that lady because you were envious of her husband's career and his status in life?"

The ill man smiled slightly as he remembered the look on the fellow's arrogant face when the prick entered his bedroom and found his wife beneath Justin. *I showed him that his fancy car and his prestigious job didn't make him a better man. Well, he didn't actually see it, but he sure 'nough heard what I had to say through his wife's screams of pleasure.*

Justin quickly removed the smile from his face and looked over at the woman suspiciously. "How do you know about that?"

"What don't I know about you?" she asked as she stood up and waltzed over to the hospital bed where a confused Justin lay. Her red heels click-clacked on the linoleum floor. "Your sins stain your soul and they're visible to anyone who cares to look."

"But you need not worry yourself about how I gained my knowledge. What you need to concern yourself with is the fact that our little sexual romp you enjoyed so much was actually a ritual," she said as she ran her hand over his body lightly. "A rite in which all of your sinful qualities were exponentially increased. The spell was completed once we reached our climaxes. It was at that point that you began your journey to become a mindless creature enslaved to those seven deadly sins I mentioned.

"You're becoming a zombie, Mr. Burrows. Soon you'll be a beast full of rage. Your lust for flesh will take on a whole new meaning and your hunger will never be sated. Of course you know how the other traits fit a zombie. Your speed will become slothful, you'll envy the living, and your vanity will keep you hidden in the shadows, afraid to come into the light lest someone lay eyes on your horrible features."

"Why...why are you doing this? You don't have to do this," Justin desperately pleaded with the woman. The whole thing seemed far-fetched to him, but who was he to deny her words. How else could he explain his current situation?

She looked down at the man with an expression of mock sympathy. "Oh, but I do have to do this. Satan demands that I send him souls and like a good little minion, I always fill my quota. Of course your miserable soul is not enough, but you're helping in your own little way. You passed the disease to your beautiful wife. She, in turn, passed it on to her mystery lover."

"What?"

"Aw, you didn't know? A woman like that couldn't sit around all alone without having her desires met, and you sure weren't taking care of home. Yep, she passed it on and he'll pass it on to another. And I haven't been idle in the least. I discovered that I can secure more souls if I complete the ritual without leaving the club. Humans can be so accommodating."

"I'll find a way to beat this," Justin declared. He refused to believe that the only thing left for him to do was lay on his deathbed. "If there's a curse then there's a counter curse...or something. There's a way to defeat this thing."

"And that's why I'm here," the woman replied. The tone of her voice suddenly changed from mocking to exasperated. "There are certain 'guidelines' set forth by Heaven that we all must abide by, and when I say 'we' I'm referring to the denizens of Hell. In order to steal souls the way I do, I am instructed to give you mortals a fighting chance. Therefore, I'm here to tell you how to defeat the zombie curse. The first thing you should know is that the first one infected within a given area is the only one who can defeat the spell."

"And...am I the first one infected?" Justin asked hopefully.

She nodded her head. "Yes, you are my first...in a manner of speaking. You're the only one who can save the soon-to-be zombies and the thousands of victims that will litter the streets of Alabama, but there's a catch."

Of course there is, Justin thought, *but I'm willing to do whatever it takes.*

"Unlike the other zombies, you have an expiration date. Ninety-six hours after the completion of the spell to be exact." The woman looked at her wristwatch. "If I'm not mistaken, you only have sixty-four hours left before Master calls you home."

"You couldn't have told me sooner?" Justin asked as he sat up in bed.

"I already told you that I've been busy."

"Well, let's not waste any more of my time. Tell me how to break the zombie curse."

The woman nodded her head. "Fair enough. In order for you to break the spell, you have to call me by my full name. The first step in the zombie curse was for me to tell you my name when we initially met. My complete name spoken by the first one infected is the only way to save yourself and everyone else."

She leaned forward seductively and whispered into Justin's ear, "Say my name."

Justin suddenly despaired. *Oh! God help me! What did she say her name was?* He shut his eyes tightly and tried to remember that moment. He could remember the flashing lights, he envisioned the writhing bodies all over the club, he knew the exact song that the DJ happened to be playing at that moment, and he remembered…her thighs.

He opened his eyes and with a forlorn expression, he stared up at the woman.

"My job here is done. Good luck to you, Justin Burrows," the lady said as she stood up straight. She smiled triumphantly then headed for the door. Before leaving the room, she turned around and said, "And you might want to have a look at yourself in the mirror. I'm sure you've been too busy to care about your appearance, but you don't look so hot."

64:08 hrs

Shortly after the woman with no name left, Justin stumbled into his tiny restroom and fumbled for the light switch. "What's her face" had been correct when she said that he hadn't had time to look in a mirror. So many other things had demanded his attention, now he was curious to see what he looked like.

The lone halogen bulb flickered on and cast a faint, yellow glow on the room. Justin staggered over to the sink and gazed into the mirror.

"No," he whispered as he ran his hands across his prune like face. "Why me, Lord?"

There appeared to be no meat on his face, or on any other part of his body. Justin was nothing but skin and bones, literally. The man's wavy hair had fallen out in patches. His eyes seemed to have withdrawn further into his sockets, and his skin clung to his now prominent bone structure. All of his beloved muscles were gone. He looked like a tall, veteran drug addict.

When did I lose teeth, Justin wondered as he inspected the inside of his mouth.

Unable to look at his reflection any longer, the terrified man turned from the mirror. *There has to be a way for me to find out that woman's name! Think,* he told himself. Justin stood there on unsteady legs for several minutes before an idea came to him. *She came to visit me! In order for them to let her in, she had to have signed some kind of visitor log. I just have to find that sheet and read off it.*

After discovering a solution, a hopeful Justin hurried out of the restroom. "Nurse!" he yelled as he lurched for the large, wooden door that barred entry to his hospital room. "Nurse! I need to find out the name of my visitor!"

Justin slowly made his way out of his room and into the hallway. "Nurse! I need some—"

"YOU!"

Justin reflexively turned to the angry shout and caught sight of a PCT pushing a wheelchair up the hall. There was a woman seated in the wheelchair and it was her who called out to him. "Talisha!" he cried out in shocked.

"You down low motherfucker!" his wife screamed. All the patients and staff who happened to be in the large corridor turned to look at the altercation. The entire seventh floor came to a standstill.

"Uh...I don't—"

"Look at you, all scrawny and sick!" she spat at him. "Here I am thinking you were out sleeping around with other women and you been with other men!"

Shocked and more than a little embarrassed, Justin glanced around at the onlookers then turned his attention back to his wife. "I ain't been sleeping with no men! I'm straight!"

"The hell you is! Look at you! You got that sickness and now you done gave it to me! YOU SHOULD'VE TOLD ME! Instead I had to find out by sitting on the toilet and have all my ...my plumbing fall into the commode water!"

"I'm sorry about you being...spayed," Justin said as he slowly retraced his steps back to his room. He stuck his head back out into the hallway and glanced at the spectators. "I ain't gay," he said hurriedly then disappeared into his room and shut the door.

"YOU BRING YOUR ASS BACK OUT HERE!"

51:50 hrs

The day became chaotic as more hysterical people arrived at the hospital holding their reproductive organs in their hands. Hospital rooms were quickly filled. Panicked, medical personnel hustled about the building without the faintest clue as to what was causing the epidemic. With Justin being the initial case, the man was caught in the midst of the chaos and never found another opportunity to search for the visitor sheet.

First, he was whisked away in a wheelchair to have more testing done. Once again, the man was poked, prodded, and questioned for hours. Around noon, the Alabama National Guard showed up and quarantined the building. No one was allowed in or out of Mercy Hospital, and the decaying individuals were confined to their rooms.

After the tests were done and the results came back, a doctor came to visit Justin.

"Mr. Burrows," the physician uttered through his face mask. "We can't find the cause for your illness. This is something never before seen in the history of mankind! I mean, all of your vital organs have shriveled up and are no longer functioning, and yet you're still...here by some miracle! You've wasted away because your muscles and soft tissues have decayed, your skin has a deathly pallor to it now, and your severe headache seems to be caused by a brain hemorrhage. And I must say, any kind of surgery seems futile at this point. It's like...you're already dead; as if you've been dead and buried for years!"

Justin shrugged his shoulders as if to say, "Oh well." He could no longer speak. At some point during the day, his tongue had fallen out of his mouth. His hopes of surviving the curse were dashed as soon as his tongue fell into his lap.

"I'm sorry, Mr. Burrows, we've done all we can."

Justin smiled at the doctor to let the guy know that he understood, but his intent was not received. Justin no longer had any lips either.

48:31 hrs

Terrible hunger pangs caused Justin to wake in the middle of the night. He looked over at the IV drip set up for him by one of the PCTs. The useless item caused him to growl out of pain and frustration, and he proceeded to rip the tube from his arm. Justin laid there for quite some time thinking about his predicament. He had to accept the fact that he was no longer a man. After all, he had been declared dead by a certified doctor.

If I could only turn back the hands of time, Justin thought. *Just a few days ago, I was normal and curse free. It was just a few days ago, but it seems so far away and beyond my grasp. If I had it all to do over again, I would do so many things differently.*

Justin thought about Talisha sitting in that wheelchair screaming at him. "So many things…" he muttered to himself. He allowed a few tears to fall from his eyes then he wiped them away. Crying would do him no good, his life was over. Even if there was a way for him to learn the woman's name, he had no tongue to speak with.

A distinct sound interrupted his thoughts. Justin's head turned to the left when he heard a cart being pushed down the hall. *There is no redo, or a video game continue. There is no going back, only forward.* He listened to the rickety cart as it came closer. *Only forward.*

"UGGGGGGGGGHHHHHHH!" the starving man moaned in an attempt to catch the attention of whoever happened to be in the hall. "UGGGGGGGGGHHHHHHHH!"

It wasn't long before the door to his room creaked open and a bit of light spilled in from the hallway. "Is everything okay in here?" a young lady asked.

"UGGGGGGGGGHHHHHHHH!" When Justin moaned for the third time, he was no longer in his hospital bed.

The woman looked out into the hallway, but there was no one there. *Nurses and PCTs ain't never where they're suppose to be,* she fussed to herself. Because she cared too much for her own good, the woman stepped into the room.

The heels of her shoes clopped on the floor as she passed the empty hospital bed. The further she went into the room, the more distance she put between her and the door, and the darker it became. She hurried over to the shadows where Justin lay on the floor groaning. It appeared as if he had fallen and was unable to climb to his feet.

"I'm not a nurse," the woman said as she came closer. "I'm a pharmacy technician delivering medicine to this floor, but I'm going to help you get into your bed, then I'll go and get a nurse."

Justin groaned in reply.

"Alright, let's get you up," she said as she bent down and grabbed the man around his waist.

Instead of climbing to his feet, he took hold of her head. Before she could scream for help, Justin snapped her neck with what little strength he had left. Her limp body fell onto the floor and the desperate man began to gorge on her flesh and wash it down with her blood. The room was filled with a sound similar to that of hogs at a feeding trough. Surprisingly, Justin could feel his strength returning as he sated his hunger.

That was just the beginning of the gruesome bloodbath that would take place at Mercy Hospital.

00:09 hrs

Many harrowing tales would be told about the two days that followed. Some had tragic endings, others less disastrous, but none had happy conclusions. The hospital staff and uninfected patients were caught unawares when the zombies rose up and began their onslaught. The victims were unarmed and their struggles were pointless. Eventually, the army did enter with their fire power, but the multiplied undead force was too much to stand against. The unholy creatures swept the soldiers aside and made a gory mess of things.

There were some among the living who put up a valiant fight in an attempt to escape Mercy Hospital. One group in particular made a historic stand. Seven survivors banded together and fought their way through the zombie horde. Only two out of that odd array ever saw the outside of Mercy Hospital. However, the pair survived only to become overwhelmed by the zombies that walked the streets of Birmingham. The story of the seven survivors is one of suspense and action, but it is not the one which matters most at the moment. Justin had nothing, or very little to do with their tale.

During those two days of murder and mayhem, Justin Burrows lost himself. His desire for revenge and flesh was never slaked, despite the numerous body counts that he managed to accumulate. After feeling like his situation was useless, Justin gave the seven deadly sins free reign and the emotions wasted little time in consuming what was left of his humanity. It was on the evening of the second day that Justin's soul was ripe for the picking.

Nine minutes remaining...

A group of special ops entered the hospital. There were ten of them, a gathering of both men and women. The trained assassins were dressed in all black and armed to the teeth. The government had received information from an anonymous source that the cure for the zombie epidemic sweeping across Alabama was located in Mercy Hospital—later known as ground zero.

Eight minutes remaining...

Special Agent Sparks made his way down the dim corridor. Dead bodies littered the hall. Some of the corpses wore hospital scrubs, there were some in hospital gowns, a couple in security guard outfits, and a large number wore digital fatigues. The dead that lay at his feet did not concern him. Sparks was more focused on the dead bodies that moved about.

The wary agent glanced around at all the blood that covered the walls, floor and ceiling. The lights overhead flickered on and off, while others were out completely. The agent moved slowly so he didn't come up on anything unexpectedly.

Seven minutes remaining...

There was static on his radio and the voice of his commander came through. "Sparks, what's your location?"

The man reached for his two-way radio while keeping his eyes on his sector. "Sarge, this is Sparks. I'm currently on the seventh floor. Everything seems…wait a minute, Sarge. I think I hear something."

Six minutes remaining…

Special Agent Sparks heard a weird sound over the normal noise of sparking wires and dripping blood. It was a loud, infamous crunching sound. He quickly raised his weapon into the firing position before continuing down the hall. Eventually, he came to a door where the sound seemed to be originating from.

Five minutes remaining…

Sparks took a deep breath to steady his nerves then he shoved the door open. The soldier entered the room with practiced precision. He checked his right, then he checked his left. Everything was clear. He walked toward the middle of the room where a curtain divided the area. The sound was coming from behind the cloth partition. Special Agent Sparks swept the curtain back.

A female zombie looked up from feasting on a dead body. It saw the armed soldier and let out a ghastly howl.

POW-POW! Sparks fired two shots at the zombie's head and the monster fell back. The agent walked over to where the creature lay and he fired another shot to ensure that the creature would never move again.

Four minutes remaining…

Once again, Sparks took a deep breath. The whole expedition was a strain on the poor man's nerves. If he was to list his top ten fears, zombies would be number three. There were numerous things about the creatures that qualified them to appear on his list of fears. He hated the way the undead creatures lurched about, and a person could never be sure when a zombie was preparing to pounce from the darkness. Last, but certainly not least, was the monsters' horrible visages. The grotesque faces that he had seen would forever haunt his dreams.

Three minutes remaining…

"Sarge, this is Sparks. I encountered a zombie, but I neutralized the—"

His transmission was interrupted when "fear number three" crept up on him and clamped its jaws on his neck. Special Agent Sparks resorted to his military training, and with a well placed chop, he was able to dislodge the beast.

Two minutes remaining...

Justin stumbled back then let out a bone chilling howl. Dry blood-caked the side of his fearsome maw and dotted the slashed military uniform that he currently wore. Acquiring the digital fatigue outfit was Justin's last rational act, before he was lost to the curse forever. He had used the uniform to infiltrate a pocket of resistance put up by a well-trained group of soldiers.

Special Agent Sparks lifted his weapon, but before he could fire, the zombie launched at the man and knocked the weapon upward. Bullets flew from the muzzle and riddled the ceiling with holes. Plaster showered the pair.

One minute remaining...

Justin wrestled the weapon from the frightened soldier and slung it across the room. With unfathomable strength gained from his constant feeding, the monster lifted Sparks into the air by his neck and slammed him against the concrete wall. The agent was so busy with trying to breath, that defending himself was the farthest thing from his mind at that point.

Zero...

All of a sudden, there was a sound at the door. Justin turned his head just in time to see someone fire three shots into his skull. His time had ran out.

Justin dropped to the floor and Sparks fell immediately after. The grateful man gasped for air.

Sergeant Rodriguez, the leader of their mission, strolled over to the hurt agent. "Did he bite you?" Rodriguez asked calmly.

"Yeah...he got a good chunk...of my neck before I could fight...him off."

Without hesitation, Sergeant Rodriguez aimed his weapon at the agent's head and fired three more shots. Special Agent

Sparks fell over dead. The leader of the expedition turned his back to the gruesome scene and grabbed his radio.

"Sparks is dead. I repeat Sparks is dead. Let's hurry up and find that damn cure so we can get out of here."

00:00 hrs

Somewhere in Atlanta, Georgia, a young man by the name of Chris Jones was at a nightclub debating on whether he should go home or not. News concerning the events in Alabama had not yet reached the rest of the states. The government kept things nice and quiet while they moved to quickly restore a semblance of order. Therefore, the inhabitants of Georgia went about their normal routines, ignorant of the horrors that existed just next door.

"You know what?" Chris said to his friend. "I think I'm just gonna go home and spend the rest of the night with my ol' lady. Ain't nothing popping off tonight."

"Ain't nothing—man, look over there at the dance floor," Mike insisted.

Chris turned from the bar and looked to where his friend was indicating. The man took a slow swig from his beer bottle as he watched a light-skinned woman dance seductively to the music. Her movements were like that of a snake charmer; hypnotizing any man who happened to look her way. The lady's tight, red dress left little to the imagination and that was beneficial for one as dense as Chris. His eyes took in her beautiful face, and proudly displayed cleavage. The man licked his lips as his sights took in her thin waist, plump bottom, and finally…her sensual thighs.

"Damn," Chris muttered. Strong, sexual urges bubbled up within the man and there was only one way to extinguish the fire that burned within his loins. He took one last sip from his bottle then sat it on the counter. "Aye, I'll see you later."

"Ai'ight then!" Mike said with a laugh as he patted Chris on the back. "Go head and handle your business, boy!"

Chris strolled across the club, seeing nothing but the woman in the red dress. The colorful lights flashed all around him. The DJ's next selection got the man's adrenaline pumping and he used that sensation to increase his courage as he approached the woman. He weaved through the dancing people with a one track mind and halted right behind the lady in red. Without looking, she backed her bottom up against his crotch and started grinding. His nature began to rise.

Chris looked back at the bar with an expression of surprise. Mike gave his friend a quiet standing ovation.

The woman leaned back so her face was close to his and she said something that Chris was unable to hear over all the music. He thought it might have been her name, he wasn't sure. "How about we go somewhere that's a little more...calm?" Chris asked loudly.

She turned to face him and smiled slyly. "I'd like that."

Termination Papers

By Suzanne Robb

Jerrod Howlins sat in his office and tapped a pen on his desk. The paperwork in front of him covered in confidential stamps, with several lines blacked out. He got the gist of it though. The government was looking for something to create a super-soldier. They wanted an *inoculation* they could provide to troops on the frontline under the guise of protecting them.

The goal of *Project Re-Genesis* was to alter the internal structures of the human body so when an injury occurred, the body would be able to heal itself within mere seconds.

Jerrod knew they meant well, but he didn't think they had the interests of the soldiers at heart. First, they planned to inoculate the soldiers without telling them. Secondly, the kind of alterations happening would be painful and most likely result in the death of some. What they were asking his company to do, would be an alteration of human DNA.

When Jerrod tried to bring these points up, General Thorne, the man in charge of the project, paid him a personal visit. In very certain and specific terms, Jerrod had been told he would either agree to work on the project, or they would ensure his company failed. The military didn't have time to deal with a squeamish business man who never saw battle. Jerrod thought about the parting words of the General,

"Perhaps when you see your friends holding their guts, you'll see the benefits of what I am trying to do."

Now, as Jerrod sat in his office looking over the last batch of test results, he cringed. The government would send him yet another thinly veiled threat, and he would respond with

53

something about having better results next time. He would be lying of course, but they didn't know that, yet.

***

Spencer Logan grabbed his coat and went to the front door. He kissed his wife Jen on the forehead, then leaned down to kiss his baby girl Lisa. Lastly he knelt down in front of his three-year-old Mike.

"Ready to protect the family while I'm gone?" Spence put a serious look on his face.

"Yes, sir, daddy sir." Mike lifted his hand to salute, and in an effort to make a serious face ended up with a scrunched up look.

Spence had to laugh. "Good, I'll be back later to take over."

He stood up and ran out the door. As usual he would have to race to work. He couldn't afford to be late again, they would fire him, and the place he worked had a unique definition of the word fire. They actually preferred the word 'terminate' for obvious reasons.

"Spence, honey, can you grab some milk on your way home tonight?" Jen waved at him to get his attention.

Spence debated just getting in the car, ignoring her. He hated stopping on the way home. After he worked a twelve hour shift dealing with unstable viruses, man-made pathogens, and animal test subjects, all he wanted to do was go home and check on the safety of his family. Looking through the window at Jen, he couldn't resist her smile. He nodded in agreement then pulled out of the driveway.

On the drive to work Spence thought about the lack of developments in his project. He and his team had been working on a serum for the government. They wanted to create a super-soldier, a man or woman who didn't need to worry about injury, not necessarily immortal, but close enough to it.

Spence kept running into the same problem. When the serum reached animal testing stages the first time, they died within moments of the injection. If death were the only issue, Spence might have slept at some point during the last few months. Instead, his head had been loaded full of images of the animals when they came back to life.

They were different from before. Their eyes were red in color, and they continued to decompose unless fed meat. Though, the meat just seemed to slow the rate of decomposition. Spence's team had tried variations on diet, but the re-animated animals only wanted meat, the fresher the better. Eventually, they were incinerated when Spence learned everything he could from them.

Spence realized the blood samples of the re-animated test subjects held only dead cells. Nothing about them was alive, not their heart, lungs, or blood. The only organ to show minimal activity was the brain, but it only lasted a few seconds. For the second batch, Spence altered the amount of immuno-suppressors thinking it would solve the problem.

When the test subjects were injected with this version they didn't start to die until the twelve hour mark. Spence watched in horror as they had seizures, choked to death on their own vomit, or simply fell over dead. He waited over two hours to see if they would re-animate, but nothing happened. He called in the disposal unit which took the bodies down to the incinerator. There they began to re-animate. Eating one another and attacking one another. Spence learned what he could from the video footage and bloody remains. The guards had no choice but to protect themselves from the crazed creatures.

Spence knew part of the process would be death, the only way for the body to alter the DNA without having the subject suffer incredible pain. After the alteration completed, the organism would re-animate stronger and better, though things hadn't been working out so far. With the third batch of the serum Spence increased the levels of plasma, and a special mix to accelerate red blood cell growth.

The test subjects were injected and after twenty-four hours were still alive. Spence monitored them carefully, terrified one would escape, or one of his team or himself might be bitten while they gathered blood and tissue samples. The ramifications of which he could only assume would be bad.

At the forty-two hour mark the animals began to twitch and screech in pain. Spence watched as his project fell over dead once again. Re-animation time quicker this time, under ten minutes. However, what they saw just beyond the observation window, unlike anything they had ever seen before.

The animals were attacking and eating one another, but weren't dying. Spence watched in amazement as each animal suffered a mortal wound only to rise up and attack another. The sight gruesome at best, gave him hope he was on the right track. All he had to do now was find a way to stop the primal instincts, and regenerate the wounds they received.

When the animals began to beat against the door and window Spence called in the clean-up unit to take care of them. Each animal had been chained to a spot on the floor providing enough room for the men to enter and put the poor creatures out of their misery. This time however the usual humane methods didn't work. The dart gun to put them to sleep had no effect, nor did the gas. They discovered the only way to kill them was to stop all brain function.

When word got out, the government threatened to pull their funding, claiming they were not going to waste tax payer dollars killing animals which came back to life as carnivorous monsters.

Spence got called into his boss's office when the announcement came down. He remembered as if it were yesterday.

***

Spence sat in the ornate waiting room for his appointment with Mister Howlins. He had been working here for ten years on small projects, all of which had been successful. This would be the first time he met his boss under less than prime circumstances.

The phone on the secretary's desk beeped, she tapped a switch and spoke into the earpiece she wore.

"Yes, sir, I'll send him right in."

"Doctor Logan, he'll see you now."

Spence took a deep breath, straightened his tie and walked over to the door. A nearby sensor caused the door to open slowly, exposing the vast office of his boss a few inches at a time.

"Spencer, sit down. I know you've heard by now we're going to lose this contract unless you have a breakthrough. None of this re-animated monkey crap."

Spencer looked at his boss, Jerrod Howlins, in his fifties, fit, very wealthy, and at the moment very unhappy. He wore a tailored grey suit, and played with his goatee as he spoke.

"Mister Howlins, I understand, but the serum isn't ready for human trials. You said it yourself, all we have is re-animated monkeys eating each other. The same thing would likely happen to humans, maybe worse."

Spence watched as his boss got up from his desk and walked to the window.

"Spencer, I built this company from the ground up. Fact is, this recession is killing me. If we don't follow through on this contract I'll be bankrupt in four months."

Spence stood still, knowing what would happen next, his boss would make a threat of some kind, thinking it would make Spence come up with a miracle at the eleventh hour.

"Mister Howlins, there's nothing I can do."

He watched his boss turn around, a flash of anger in his eyes. "I didn't hire you to hear you say you can't do something. I hired you because you were the top of your class in bioengineering, and came highly recommended. You have three months to get the serum working, or you'll get your *termination papers*."

"Yes, sir." Spence swallowed audibly.

"Now, get the hell out of my office and start putting your genius brain to work "

Spence stood up and nearly ran out of the office. A part of him wanted to go home and pack up his family. Change their names and never look back, though he knew his boss or the government would find him eventually.

***

That had been two and a half months ago, and Spence had tested eighteen variations of the serum since then, with the resulting death of one hundred and eighty seven test subjects. Though the last batch of subjects had lived almost forty-eight hours before they died, then re-animated into flesh eating monsters.

Spence pulled into the parking lot and showed his identification to the guard on duty. Then followed the painted lines until he got to the parking garage where he punched in his personal code. Grabbing his laptop and briefcase, he exited the car and went to the elevator.

Here, he had to pass a retinal scan, once inside the elevator, he placed his finger on a small pad which took a DNA sample as well as matching his fingerprint. The elevator began to move, opening a minute later to reveal his lab. The security here top notch, the military had made sure of it. Spence wondered if they wanted to keep the wrong people out, or the right people in.

The fact the military ran the place motivated Spence to work his ass off. On a project like this, *termination papers* meant you had a car accident on the way home, or perhaps a heart attack, no matter what, the threat crystal clear.

He sat at his desk with a sigh. Looking over the latest results he could see three out of four specimens from the batch injected yesterday were still alive. He pressed a button for a clean-up tech to remove the deceased animal. Spence hated when they re-animated, and tried to avoid it at all costs.

The doors hissed open, and Spence almost jumped out of his seat when Greg Miller tapped his shoulder. He'd assumed the clean-up tech entered.

"Geez, Spence, why so jumpy?" Greg went to his lab table and set down a cup of coffee and bag of doughnuts.

"I thought you were here for the body." Spence pointed to the corpse, the other three animals circling it.

"Ah, that's right you hate when they come back," Greg chuckled.

"You think it's funny to watch an animal suffer? To come back as some sort of thing we created? A monster plain as day and you can laugh?" Spence shook with anger.

Greg's eyes went wide. "Sorry, Spence, I don't think it's funny, but when you work in a place like this, if you take it too seriously it'll make you crazy."

"I don't care, show some respect." Spence flipped open his laptop and planned on ignoring Greg for the rest of the day.

Why didn't it work? All the compounds were right, the calculations and measurements accurate. Where did he go wrong? Spence had tried various animals to see if the problem might be species related. He got his answer, every animal from mouse to horse died, then re-animated with his serum.

Spence began to go crazy. He had days left to get a working serum, or he would get his *termination papers*. He worked for hours, and only looked up when Greg buzzed him.

"What?" Spence had found something and didn't want to be disturbed.

"Do you want me to call clean-up? The other three died a few minutes ago."

Spence looked into the containment chamber; sure enough, the other three were all dead. Looking over at Greg, he nodded, then went back to work. He'd been basing the measurements of compounds to use in the serum, based on the average number of red and white blood cells in humans. Not to mention the levels of immuno-suppressors he had been adding.

No wonder it didn't work, a mouse certainly didn't have the same amount as a human did. Spence looked up from his calculations and yelled at Greg.

"Hey, come over here, I think I might have something."

Spence smiled as Greg hurried over to him. This might just work, they just had to readjust the levels and try it on a new batch.

"What is it? What did you find?"

Spence pointed to the screen which had all the data they had been using to make the serum. He wanted to see if it stuck out like a sore thumb to Greg, too. After a few moments Greg shook his head.

"Look at the red and white blood cell levels." Spence leaned away from his monitor as Greg leaned in.

"Holy crap, no wonder everything went wrong."

"Exactly, we were prepping it for human use, but we forgot to take into consideration the red and white blood cell counts. Too much serum would override the red blood cells causing too much oxygen to flow into the system, and the organism would exhaust itself fighting against the immuno-suppressors trying to create white blood cells to fight off what they consider a foreign invader."

"Okay, death gets explained by this. The animals we tested had no live blood cells, but what about the re-animation?" Greg asked.

"I have no idea, but this is a new way to go. We have less than two weeks Greg, it's do or die time."

Greg went over to the white board and began putting new numbers in the equation. Spence went over, too, correcting errors and making new calculations in his head. Three hours later they had an entirely new compound, they just had to synthesize it into a serum.

"Greg, set up the computer with these numbers, get the serum made. Should be done in about two hours, I'll be back. Need to go home for a bit, I think this is going to be a long night."

Greg just nodded as he entered the new values into the columns of the machine they used to create the sample compounds.

Spence felt a weight lift off his shoulders. He felt confident he had solved the problem. Finally, he could breathe. Heading down to the parking garage he felt a noticeable lift in his step. He even remembered to stop for milk, and didn't get annoyed.

When he arrived home, he sat in his driveway for a few moments staring at his house. Hopefully things would be back to normal soon and he would actually get to spend some time with his family. The house was dark, but he knew Jen would be up waiting for him. He grabbed his briefcase and went inside.

"Hi, honey, I'm home," he said in a sing-song voice; he just felt so damn good.

"Hey there, handsome, you're sure in a good mood." Spence tossed his briefcase on the floor, hung up his coat, and went into the kitchen.

Jen stood in front of the stove and Spence walked up behind her. She was so beautiful, and for reasons unknown, she actually loved him. Wrapping his arms around her, he inhaled the smell of her hair. Strawberries, he loved the smell.

"Had a good day at work, actually still working, but I needed to come home and see you and the kids before I did anything else." He backed up when she gently nudged him with her hips.

"Really? Do you have to go back in tonight?" Jen had kept a plate warming in the oven for him, roast beef with peas and mashed potatoes, his favourite.

"I do, honey, but soon things will calm down. It's just we're in creation phase, so we have to run so many tests." Spence went to the table and sat in front of the food she set out for him.

"I don't know why you work there. You can get a better job that actually appreciates you. You look so tired, Spence, I'm worried."

Spence looked up from the mouthful of food he'd prepared. He noticed Jen had frown lines, and worry marks covering her face. When did those happen? He rested his hand on the table and looked at her in what he hoped she interpreted as reassuring.

"Jen, I promise this will pay off. Everything I'm doing is for you and the kids. You guys are my life. Everything will be okay I promise."

Spence relaxed as she smiled at him. He ate with gusto listening to her talk about her day. She filled him in on what Mike, their three-year-old had gotten up to in the bathroom with the bubbly soap. Then he sighed as she told him their nine-month-old daughter Lisa had tried to take a few steps. She was going to be a fast learner like her daddy.

"Honey, an amazing dinner as usual. I don't deserve you." Spence leaned back in his chair and patted his non-existent belly.

"Whatever. Let me clean this up. Go and give the kids a kiss, I know you're dying to."

"You know me too well." Spence got up heading out of the kitchen.

"Don't you forget it."

Spence laughed as he made his way up the stairs. He went to Mike's room first. He knelt next to the bed, tucking the blanket more securely around his son.

"Love you, kiddo, if everything goes right tonight, I'm actually going to get to spend some time with you. Maybe we can to the museum next weekend."

Spence got up slowly and kissed his son on the cheek. He crept out of the room and went into Lisa's nursery. She snored softly, and he placed his hand on her back and made small circular motions.

"Hey, baby girl, daddy loves you. I want to see your first step, so I have to go back into work tonight and get lots of stuff done." He leaned down and gave her a kiss on her fuzzy head.

Walking out of the nursery Spence felt a chill dance up and down his spine. He looked around for the cause of the draft, but found nothing. He shrugged it off, nothing would ruin his mood. Spence was confident he'd solved the problem, or at least very, was close to a solution.

Back in the kitchen he sat with Jen for a few minutes chatting before getting ready to leave. When he stood up Jen stopped him. She gave him a kiss, long a deep. The warmth of her body pushing away the coldness he felt earlier. He could be a few minutes late, Greg was there after all.

An hour later, Spence ran out the door, a smile on his face. As he started his car he waved to Jen who stood in the window. All the way to work he couldn't stop smiling. When he pulled into the parking lot and showed his identification he practically whistled.

In the elevator he could feel his body start to hum with excitement. The discovery, the solved problem, an absolute high for Spence. He knew they'd cracked a big part of the mystery tonight, he hoped it would be enough.

Entering the lab he saw Greg holding a vial. Spence got butterflies in his stomach. He felt like a virgin on prom night. Would it happen tonight?

"How does it look?" Spence walked over to Greg and took the vial.

"Looks like it was ready an hour ago, where were you? Are we ready to do this?" Greg's obvious excitement took any anger from his words away.

"I'm ready. Let's get this done." Spence loaded the vial full of serum into an injector.

"I had four subjects sent up." Greg went to grab the injector.

Spence shook his head. "No, I got it this time."

Greg looked at him oddly.

"I know, I usually don't do this part, but it feels right this time." Spence entered the room and injected each one of the animals.

They were chained to the floor, but he still had to be careful to avoid bites, nips, and a few grabs. Injections done, he exited the room. The doors hissed shut behind him.

"Now we wait." Greg grabbed a stool and placed it in front of the window to the specimen room.

Spence sighed, he felt so relaxed. This had to work; it felt so right this time. He went to the window and stood watching.

Three hours later, no visible change in the specimens had occurred. Spence drank his fourth cup of coffee and ate a stale Danish. Glancing at the monitors, he could see all body rhythms were normal. So far…so good.

A low beeping woke Spence. He looked around to try and determine the cause. The inside of the specimen room looked like it had been painted completely red. He ran to the window and looked in. Three of the subjects appeared to have been ripped apart, and partially eaten. The sole survivor sitting there, bits of fur and flesh hanging out of its teeth.

Spence hit the window with his hand. "Damn it! I thought we had it this time."

"What happened?" Greg, woken up by Spence's outburst, approached the window.

"I'll tell you what happened, we failed. Take a look. Might as well run now before they find out." Spence started to panic, if his boss found out about this he would get his *termination papers*.

Greg went to the computers and began to replay the taped material on the monitors. While they slept one of the subjects started to convulse and throw up a reddish substance, very much resembling blood.

The other three animals screeched in fear as they tried to pull at the chains in order to get away from the sick one.

The one convulsing fell over, apparently dead. The others screeched even more, and began to claw around their necks to try and free themselves. Spence had never seen such a reaction before. Moments later the one which keeled over started to move, the others animals letting out primal sounds of fear and rage.

As the one rose up from the ground, Spence noted it was different than the other re-animates they'd dealt with. This one had milky eyes, and the monitors picked up minimal brain function, something the others didn't have. He also realized this particular one had a preference for brains, something else new.

Spence had to look away as the animal attacked with quick and efficient moves, pinning his victim to the ground then beating their head on the floor until it cracked like a coconut. Once open he ate large chunks of the brain. The other two watched quietly knowing their fate.

The animal almost took less than fifteen minutes to pin the other ones individually, and open their heads like melons. After they were pinned the *thing*—as Spence thought of it—moved around aimlessly. Playing with some of the organs in the bodies of the others, gnawing on a few bones, but for the most part more interested in the door. This one was stronger and more intelligent than its predecessors.

Spence, in full panic mode wanted to delete the video coverage. He also needed to clean up the mess in the specimen room. Without thinking he grabbed the gun to kill the *thing* he'd created, and entered the room.

He raised the gun to fire, but realized he'd made a fundamental error. The *thing* had not only broken free of its chains, but had been studying the door. Spence watched in slow motion as it ran straight for him and sank its teeth deep into his thigh. He cried out in pain and brought the butt of the gun down on the *thing's* head.

The strike did no damage; it didn't even seem to faze the *thing*. Spence continued to hit it as Greg tried using one of the electrical prods they had. Finally, Spence took control of himself, and pointed the gun at the monster's head.

"Greg, back up you don't want this to get on you." Spence pulled the trigger and hoped he didn't shoot himself in the foot.

The monster fell to the ground with a thud. Spence fell back against the wall grabbing his leg as blood gushed from the gaping hole the *thing* had left in it. Spence clenched his teeth at the throbbing sensation. He could feel his heartbeat in his leg with each new spurt of blood.

He'd just ruined everything. He would never see his family again, never see Lisa's first step, or help Mike with his math homework. Never again would he smell the strawberry scent of Jen's hair.

He watched in slow motion as Greg hit the alarm button. In thirty seconds a clean-up team would enter. The specimens would be destroyed, and Spence would be put under quarantine and studied.

He knew if it had been Greg, he would have killed him so he wouldn't suffer through the indignity of being put on the other side of the glass as he slowly turned into a monster.

He watched as Greg came over to him.

"Sorry, Spence, but I might be able to learn from what happens with your blood. I have a family to think about, too."

Spence nodded and saw the elevator doors open. Several men in hermitically sealed white suites entered. As they took stock of the situation, Spence tried to raise the gun to his head, but couldn't go through with it. He dropped it, letting it fall to the floor, making a loud clattering noise in the now quiet lab. One of the suited men came over to him and began an examination.

"How do you feel?"

The voice sounded far away.

"My leg is killing me and I'm tired, otherwise normal." Spence didn't want to help, but he held on to hope of a cure, or the thought that the bite had not fully infected him.

They'd readjusted the serum after all. The new one had been intended to work on small animals, not full grown men. Maybe he would just get a little sick. As unlikely a scenario it was, he needed something to hold onto.

Spence felt a pinch as one of the men in white took a sample of this blood. A scream off to his left caused him to glance over. Greg lay on the ground in a growing pool of blood. Spence had wondered if they would to do something like that, take care of a possible witness. Someone who might talk to the press, or try to black mail them with what he'd seen.

"We're taking you up to a special room," the voice was calm, collected, and unemotional.

Spence felt himself being lifted onto a gurney. He guessed they were taking him to a special wing of the facility. One they'd prepared for an occasion just like this. He would be put behind the glass, quarantined and observed.

These men in white would watch him, learn from him, then, Spence hoped to God, they would terminate him.

Once on the gurney, his *escorts* as he thought of them, took no chances. They used restraints on his wrists and ankles. He felt a belt looped around his waist, and knew then and there, he would never see his family again.

Spence felt like it took an eternity to get to the *special room*, but he had no way to gauge the time. The restraints were loosened, but not removed.

"Spencer, how do you feel?" A man in white loomed above his face.

"I feel the same as before, my leg hurts and I'm still tired. Out of curiosity is anyone going to take a look at my leg?" Spence was getting impatient, the longer they waited to look at his wound, the more chance he had of becoming infected.

"We're going to have someone look at it now, right after we give you something for the pain." Spence tried to say no, but felt the sting of a needle.

Spence ran as fast as he could, but tripped on the curb. He reached out a hand to Jen as she stood in the doorway. Baby Lisa cried in her arms, little Mike standing in front of his mother protectively. Then the thing attacked, Spence screamed as he saw his family ripped to shreds.

"No!" Spence woke up, a sheen of sweat covered him.

He tried to move, but realized the restraints were still in place. Spence lifted his head to look down at his leg. A sheet covered it, but he saw the bulge of a bandage, though it didn't mean they actually did anything to help him. They were desperate, and he knew that chances were, they would do everything they could to accelerate whatever may or may not happen to him.

"You're awake, that's good. How are you feeling?"

A man Spence had never seen before moved into his line of sight.

"Who are you? What about my leg? How long did I sleep for?" Spence wanted to ask a million more questions, but the man raised a hand.

"Calm down, don't get yourself worked up. My name is Doctor Hillary, I'm a geneticist. The military brought me in to help you. As for your leg, it looks like it's fine, no signs of infection around the bite. As for how long you have been sleeping, at least thirty-three hours."

"What? How come I slept so long? What did they give me?" Spence began to panic, but then realized he'd passed several crucial time thresholds.

Most of the other test subjects were either dead, or showing severe symptoms by this time. He let out a sigh of relief; perhaps he'd avoided infection after all. Then another thought occurred to him, what if the serum worked? What if Spence was now proof they had the ability to make a super-soldier. What would they do with him then?

"We're not sure why you slept so long, but all your blood levels are normal, as well as pulse and heart rates. You had a minor spike in temperature, but it passed. Seems like whatever you were experimenting with didn't infect you."

Spence thought about what Doctor Hillary just said.

Seems like whatever you were experimenting with didn't infect you.

The good doctor hadn't been filled in on what they were doing. Then Spence thought about the fact they'd called in a geneticist.

"Doctor Hillary, why did they call you in? What would a gene doctor want with me?"

The doctor cleared his throat. "Some of the test results were strange, they wanted me to take a look at them. I should go and let you get some rest."

"Hold on, what do you mean strange? What tests?" Spence could hear the desperation in his voice.

The serum, if it worked would have altered Spence's DNA, his red and white blood cells would work at an accelerated rate to heal any wound he suffered, including the one on his leg. If he'd succeeded, it would make sense for them to call in a geneticist to run all the required tests.

The hiss of a door shutting was the only response he would get. He lifted his head and saw the large glass wall. Spence knew there were at least two other doctors or scientists on the other side watching him.

He had to think, what else could have come back strange? Then he recalled the exact words the doctor used: blood levels. Doctor Hillary didn't say what his red or white blood cell counts were. Spence felt his heart begin to pound.

As soon it did, a monitor next to him let out several beeps. Turning his head he saw a wall of machines which had wires leading to him. He lifted his head again to look down at his leg, he needed to see the injury. He needed to know if it had healed. He tried to move his leg to see if there were any flares of pain, he sighed in relief when there wasn't even a twinge of discomfort.

He knew if he struggled they would come in and give him a sedative of some sort, or think he might be getting ready to die then re-animate. He laid his head down on the pillow and sighed.

Spence wondered if they told Jen he had died, or if she waited at home worried sick about him, wondering where he could be. He wanted to ask them, but knew he had to gain their trust. They needed to be convinced he would work with them, only then would they share information.

Thirty-three hours, he'd been asleep a long time. He had fifteen more hours to go in order to cross the time threshold none of the other test subjects had passed.

"Hey, can you at least give me a TV, or send someone in to talk to me, this is getting boring."

Spence didn't get a response. Then again he didn't expect one. He only said something to show he had the ability to organize thought, form a sentence, and overall not demonstrating signs of becoming a flesh eating monster.

Spence fell into an uneasy sleep, visions of blood and gore assaulted him. He dreamt of his wife Jen and finding her torn open completely eviscerated as their two kids sat next to her crying. He woke up with beads of sweat trailing from his forehead down his neck. He could feel the pillow beneath him was soaked.

"Hey, how long has it been now? You know if I pass the forty-eight hour mark everything is fine, right?" Once again, he just wanted to let them know he could still think and organize his thoughts.

The hissing sound of the doors opening let Spence know someone had entered the room. He turned his head to the side to see his boss, Mister Howlins. From the look on his face he couldn't tell if things were going to go bad, or get worse.

"Spence, sorry you have to go through this, protocol and whatnot." His boss stayed near the door, and avoided eye contact.

"Mister Howlins, can I talk to my wife? She must be worried sick. Not to mention, everything seems to be fine with me. I don't think the infection got me, even Doctor Hillary agrees."

"Spence, you remember the papers we had to sign when we agreed to work on this project. As dictated, if any member of the team is exposed to the serum they become property of the United States Government. Your wife was notified of your death yesterday morning, I'm sorry."

Spence hit his head against the pillow, he pulled at his restraints. Damn this stupid project, and his boss. He wanted to see his family, he needed to see them.

"You're all a bunch of bastards. So what do you have planned for me? Let me sit in here the rest of my life until I go insane with boredom? Perform tests on me until there's nothing left but a shell of a man?"

Spence heard the beeps on the machinery increase. He looked over and saw his pulse rate, one hundred and twelve, his blood pressure seventy over fifty, and his temperature a whopping one hundred and three. Crap. So it begins.

"Spence, I don't think you got out of this unscathed, we're going to keep you as comfortable as possible and try to find a cure. Doctor Hillary is going to come back in to talk to you about *Project Re-Genesis*. He's been given clearance, so you can talk with him freely about your work."

Spence watched as his boss left the room as quickly as possible. He knew why Doctor Hillary wanted to talk to him, he would be changing soon, or so they thought. Well, not if he had anything to say about it.

Spence thought hard about the changes he'd made to the new serum. He'd adjusted for lower red and white blood cells. He'd also adjusted it to use more immuno-suppressors so the white blood cells wouldn't attack the serum as it altered the DNA.

The hiss of the doors alerted him to the entrance of Doctor Hillary. He didn't bother turning his head, or even acknowledging the man. He would ask his questions, and Spence would answer them.

"Spencer, how are you feeling?" Doctor Hillary looked at the monitors and various read outs.

"Like a prisoner, how are you?" Spence turned his head when he heard the rustling of papers.

Doctor Hillary carried a file and a clipboard. This would be more than a friendly chat to see how he felt.

"I can understand that." The sound of a chair being dragged across the floor echoed in the small room.

Spence snorted. "Really? You can understand, so you're a prisoner too then. You're being held in restraints, and your family thinks you're dead?" The beeps started again on the machines.

"Spencer, you need to try and stay calm, when you get agitated you just accelerate the process."

"Process, what process? You have no idea what we've done here."

"Spencer, I have looked over most of the surveillance videos, your notes, and all the lab results for each experiment. What I can't figure out is your current situation."

Spence laughed. "What situation? I'm dead to the world."

71

"If you're going to waste my time, I can't help you. You don't seem to understand, since I last spoke to you changes started to take place on a genetic level. Your red and white blood cell counts are all over the place, your immune system is not reacting, and you're blood pressure and pulse rates are in the danger zone. Not to mention you now have a fever."

"Why won't you let me see my leg? Let me see it and I'll cooperate."

Spence watched as Doctor Hillary stood up and left the room. An eternity later he re-entered with a small mirror in his hand. He approached Spence, but this time refused to make eye contact.

Doctor Hillary pulled the sheet up from the base of the bed, then pulled the bandage off of where Spence had been bit. Whatever he expected to see, wasn't what got reflected to him in the mirror. The bite had turned into a large hole, as if they tried to dig out a portion of his leg. The area around a dark green, almost black color, pus and ooze moved around. The lower portion of his leg as well as the upper part had turned a pale green. Spence looked away from the mirror wanting to throw up.

"As you can see, Spencer, things have changed rather quickly. When I checked the wound this morning it looked healthy. I need to know what you're thinking and feeling right now. It's the only way I can help you."

Spence remained quiet. The other specimens had died, then began to decompose. Spence was beginning to rot, even though he hadn't died. He had to think, what made this serum different. Then it hit him, he almost laughed at how stupid they all were to miss the obvious.

The serum didn't make the difference, it was all about mutation. He should have thought of it sooner, it was the basis of evolution after all. His serum wasn't creating monsters, it caused an evolution of some kind, perhaps not a good one, but a possible one.

When he injected the test subject, which had been a monkey, the serum altered the DNA of the monkey. This meant when he got bit, he had been infected with an altered version of the original strain of the serum.

Like most pathogens they adapt to their environment. From the needle, to the monkey, to the man. From the serum, to blood, to saliva, to blood again. The path it followed irrelevant, the outcome the same.

Spence knew then, he would end up like his test subjects. He showed the signs of changing already. He didn't know how long it would take as he was the first human subject, he was patient zero.

"Doctor Hillary, it mutated. The serum mutated in the test subjects, something about the mutation killed them, but there was still some part of the serum that worked because they re-animated. The whole point of *Project Re-Genesis* was to help soldiers heal quickly while in the heat of battle. The serum brought the test subjects back to life, but different. They were cannibalistic monsters. Their brain activity was gone, and their organ function non-existent."

The sound of the chair being pulled close once again. "So you think the bite which infected you, had an altered version of the serum in it?"

Spence sighed, how could he explain this to a geneticist. "Think of it like this. Imagine I say something to you and you repeat it to someone else, then they repeat it and so on."

"Like the telephone game, my daughter loves to play that."

"Yes, exactly like that. The end phrase is never the one you started out with. What we're dealing with here follows the same concept. We injected a different version of the serum into the test subjects this time, one catered to their size. What we didn't know, could never have expected, is it would adapt and mutate in order to survive. When I got bit, the mutated strain of the serum passed from the saliva right into my blood..."

Spence stopped talking, he felt tired.

"Then as soon as it entered your bloodstream it began to mutate and adapt to your system. Though it doesn't explain why you're displaying signs of being infected or the necrotic tissue around the wound."

Spence let out a small laugh. "It's because I'm going to become one of them, perhaps a bit different, but I will become a cannibalistic monster. If there was a humane bone in any of your bodies, you'd kill me before it happens."

"Can you feel any changes? Is there anything different about your body?"

Spence wanted to laugh, or tell the guy off. He didn't though; instead he took stock of his body and how he felt. He definitely had a headache, and knew he had a fever, but was cold at the same time. His leg, from the looks of it should be causing him significant pain, but he felt nothing.

"Doctor Hillary, in all honesty I just feel like I have a bad flu. Fever and chills, no appetite, headache, as well as some body aches."

"Okay, Spencer, I'm going to draw some more blood samples and let you rest. I'll be back in a bit to see how you're doing."

Spencer fell asleep before the doctor had time to pick up the needle.

In his sleep, he was once again attacked with violent images of blood and gore. This time however, he was the one doing all the damage. He chased after his family and felt a rush of something primal when he heard Jen scream.

As he bit into her and felt the warm flow of her blood he groaned in delight. Then he bashed her head like he had watched the monkey do. When it finally opened he gorged himself on the pink fleshy bits of brain as they fell out.

A scream caused him to look up, little Mike was there holding Lisa. Spence began to approach them, their screams urging him on as well as the scent of fresh meat.

"*No!*" Spence woke with such force when he sat up that he broke the restraint holding his left arm in place.

He realized he now had a way out, an escape plan. He quickly put his hand back in position and hoped whoever watched on the other side of the mirror had fallen asleep, or didn't notice.

The doors hissed open and Spence saw a haggard looking Doctor Hillary enter.

"What is it? What happened?" the doctor asked.

"Dream, nightmare really…" Spence heard the beeps and blips going crazy next to him.

"Try and calm down." Doctor Hillary looked at the readouts and re-set a few of the machines.

"Trust me, doc, I'm not trying to rush things along." Spence knew time was short, if he could just get out and see his family one last time.

He just wanted to hold his baby girl and see his little boy, then take one last smell of strawberry hair. He didn't think it was a lot to ask. He closed his eyes and tried to calm his breathing.

"Spencer, are you hungry at all? You haven't eaten in almost three days."

"No, Doc, not hungry at all. Hey, what time is it anyways?"

Doctor Hillary looked down at his watch. "It's two thirty in the morning."

Spence knew if he planned to get out of here, it would have to be soon. At this hour, the security, and number of people at the lab would be minimal at best.

At that moment a pain seized Spence in the gut. He wanted to bend over, but couldn't. Doctor Hillary noticed his distress and came over to try and hold him down. Spence shut his eyes against the bright light above him then felt the gorge rise.

Blood erupted from his mouth and nose coating both him and Doctor Hillary. Spence convulsed a few times then stopped moving entirely. The machines started to beep incessantly then went silent, each screen had a flat line running across it.

***

The doors hissed open and Ted Hillary knew he would be taken to a room just like this one and strapped to a table as people watched on the other side of the mirror. He tried to fight off the men in the white suits, but there were too many of them. As he gave in, he watched in horror as the body of Spencer Logan began to rise. The left hand was free, and undid the right hand restraint, then reached down and undid the belt and ankle restraints. The men in white were apparently too stunned to move.

Ted looked into Spencer's eyes, the eyes of death. They were milky white, and dark liquid oozed out of his mouth. He got off the bed and grabbed Ted by the arm, too shocked to do anything else, he watched as the *thing* he knew as Spencer Logan bit his arm and ripped off a strip of flesh which he greedily chewed. Ted screamed and turned to the men in white suits for help.

They stood there frozen, unsure what to do.

***

Spence caught bits and pieces of what was going on. He had an insatiable hunger which needed tending. He grabbed the nearest source of meat and bit. Then he noticed bright white things moving. He ran towards them taking then down, pounded their heads onto the floor, their helmets cracking open. He leaned over each one, his bloody drool leaking in between the cracks.

He turned to look back at the first meat he ate; it was on the ground convulsing. Spence stood up and ran out of the open doors. People screamed, but he ignored them. He had somewhere to be. Loud shots were heard and he felt things hitting his body, but it didn't stop him. He bit anything near him, and soon heard the others following behind him. He needed to find strawberry hair; then, with a bloody smile. He remembered he wanted to deliver some *termination papers* to his boss.

***

Screams echoed throughout the building that night, the infection mutated so quickly that people were turned into zombies within moments of contact with any sort of fluid, or a bite. No one but the government knew how it happened or who started it, and they were not about to share the information.

In a dark room, under several locks and multiple keycard slots, a file waited. In it a single sheet of paper and photo. The paper had the words *Project Re-Genesis* written across the top, a large stamp in red ink declared it *FAILED*. A detailed picture of a DNA strand was printed on the paper, a write up claiming human trials should be put on hold.

The photograph was of a man in his mid-thirties. He had brown shaggy hair and blue eyes. He smiled lopsidedly and had deep dimples which endeared him to anyone who looked at the picture…until they saw PATIENT ZERO written across the bottom.

ZERO

The Scientific Method

By Nathaniel W. Phillips

I try to avoid watching the news these days. If there is a world-changing story, then I'll hear about it from a neighbor or at the local coffee shop. Otherwise, it probably isn't too important. You almost have to adopt that attitude once you've been working for the press long enough. The hardest thing about being on the inside is you realize how people tend to get concerned about the different stories they hear, but what they really need to worry about is everything they aren't hearing.

As they say, knowledge is power. The thing is, knowledge is worthless unless everyone knows about it. Maybe a lab developed a form of clean fuel, but it doesn't do folks any good unless they know it's available. So it's true that knowledge is power, but the real power is in the ability to disseminate that knowledge. The same groups of people within the press decide every day which pieces of knowledge everyone hears and which pieces of knowledge no one hears. The only time the press doesn't have the final say in the matter is when major governments get involved, and the only time that happens is to keep their secrets.

I was a clerk for *The Post*. I didn't do secretarial stuff all day long, but I didn't get to do the stuff that would make you Carl Bernstein or Bob Woodward either. I mainly collected information on menial stories, acting as a checker of sorts who would go from place to place to either verify facts or find new ones. I never got a shot at the glory that the investigative journalists had, but now I know that what they had was more of a curse than anything.

People tend to have misconceptions about what investigative journalists are. These are no small-town reporters. These are guys who, in a different time and place, could have been Pinkertons or, nowadays, counter-intelligence operatives. Given that, I was more than a bit surprised when my boss at the time told me that I'd be heading to Russia for about a week. I had been living for my job for about two and a half years, and it seemed like I wasn't going anywhere. I must have impressed someone, because the opportunity simply came out of the blue, but it probably helped that I speak enough Russian to order a drink.

I was told to go with Pretlow. He had been with *The Post* for a few years, and he was well established as one of the paper's top translators. Other than English, he spoke five languages like a native: Spanish, Portuguese, German, French, and Dutch. I figured that there must have been a good reason to have the two of us go together, but it wasn't obvious to me at the time. These higher-ups have a pretty good grasp on what they want, and they know which tools to use to get it.

Pretlow and I were put on a flight to St. Petersburg. They handed me an address, and my job was to go there immediately after we landed. Once we arrived at the location, I was to tell the elderly man we'd find there that we were reporters. He would give us some documents, and then we would head back to the airport to catch the next flight to Washington. It seemed like a pretty simple assignment, and in fact, it was, but the repercussions of it all…good Lord, saying that it was merely out of my league would trivialize the entire situation.

The flight was a long one with layovers in Newark and Paris. Pretlow and I were anxious to get back on the ground by the second leg of the flight. In spite of the usual noisy children, sick passengers, and sub-par food, it turned out to be a good thing to have some time to talk to Pretlow. Between chatting about past assignments and trading various stories about mutual coworkers, he filled me in on some of the details of our assignment by telling me about Dr. Edwin Fenstermacher, a young Nazi SS officer.

Fenstermacher completed his medical schooling in Germany in 1943, and because his father was a personal friend of Wilhelm Koppe, the SS commander of Poland, some strings were pulled to have the doctor placed as the head medical officer at the Gross-Rosen concentration camp in early 1944. The camp put inmates to work in the nearby stone quarry until they outlived their usefulness.

While Fenstermacher is not nearly as notorious as Dr. Josef Mengele, records show that he committed similar war crimes on a smaller scale through his experimentation on some of the prisoners. What Pol Pot was to Joseph Stalin, if you will. Dr. Fenstermacher remained at Gross-Rosen until its liberation by the Red Army in February of 1945. At that point, he fled the encroaching forces. His whereabouts were unknown until the late 1950s when he was discovered to be living in Argentina. It is unknown how long he lived there, and he disappeared shortly after the one verified account of his residence in that country surfaced. It is strongly rumored that the Israeli Mossad found him and either killed him in Argentina or forcibly extradited him to Israel where he was either executed immediately or held in captivity for a number of years first.

Pretlow also told me, in more detail than I will repeat here, of Fenstermacher's experiments. While the good doctor was not present at the hearing, formal charges from the Nuremberg Tribunal alleged that, aside from enabling mass murder, Fenstermacher committed crimes including his "studies" on the functionality of the human brain.

Pretlow claimed ignorance on the exact nature of the documents that we would be retrieving in St. Petersburg. The only thing he said was that they related to Dr. Fenstermacher in some way.

***

The beauty of historic St. Petersburg greeted us upon our arrival in the city: monuments to war heroes and leaders, unique architecture, and of course the vast cathedrals. I asked for directions from some locals, and we began our trek. However, we quickly realized that poverty still cripples modern Russia. The poor hid in the shadows of derelict buildings. We could not see their faces since most were completely covered in rags to fend off the insatiable maw of the biting cold. Skeletal dogs pawed at anything that might yield something edible. Signs on shops were so worn that they were barely legible. We kept moving until, well after dusk, we finally reached our destination: a decrepit old building with broken windows and the street urchins to match.

The rotting doorway led to a long, yellowed, and stinking hallway littered with paint chips. The bare and dripping pipes along the ceiling pointed the way to our goal. We knocked on the door, and, after a long wait, a scruffy elderly man opened the door. I explained to him that we were the reporters from *The Post.*

The small man shook my hand with an unexpectedly firm grip for his size and waved us in and over to his kitchen table. I looked around at the walls as they were the only portions of the cubby hole-sized dwelling not covered in clutter. There were various framed black and white photographs hanging in the room, all of them concerning one of two themes: a wrinkled woman with sunken eyes who did not appear to be present in the quarters, and young men in their twenties wearing military uniforms.

The old man limped to a well-worn chair and slowly took a seat. The man identified himself as Aleksandr Zamenhof. The impediment, he soon explained, was the result of a shrapnel injury he incurred while serving as a lieutenant in Stalin's Red Army. He led a platoon of rifle infantry and apparently saw a lot of action when fighting the Germans. Zamenhof worked at a factory after the war because his limp precluded him from further military service. Since then, the only significant thing that has happened to him was the passing of his wife about fifteen years ago. Otherwise, his daily routine of working at the steel mill and coming home has been going on since the end of the war over fifty years ago.

Zamenhof slowly rose from his chair and shuffled toward the stove to pour us some tea. After preparing the beverage for us, a look of concern overcame Zamenhof's face as he hobbled toward a darkened back room.

The Scientific Method

Pretlow and I sipped the diluted, lukewarm tea while the old man searched for the documents. About half an hour later, after refusing our help on multiple occasions, Zamenhof made his way back to the table. He dropped a book and various loose papers in front of us and scowled. He muttered under his breath, which sounded to me like "the things those people went through…"

Zamenhof explained that his mother was of German descent, so he was familiar with some basic German. He said that from the little bit he could read of the documents, it looked like a personal journal, and we surmised that it had belonged to Edwin Fenstermacher. He explained that it came into his possession when he and his platoon, among others, marched across Poland and found the Gross-Rosen camp deserted by the occupying Nazis. They found many dead prisoners with a handful barely alive. The Nazis had tried to cover their tracks by killing the inmates and incinerating the bodies, but they did not have time to finish either task before the Red Army approached. Zamenhof said that he discovered the officers' quarters and looked around one of the rooms. There he found a Jew in his late teens by the name of Kapler who had been rummaging around. This Kapler was ushered out to join the other refugees, but not before he took a tattered, thick notebook that was losing pages even during the commotion. Since none of the high-ranking Russian officers were present, no one gave the boy any trouble, especially considering the living conditions that were plain to everyone. Instead, Zamenhof looked through what was left of the officer's belongings himself. Finding nothing of real value, he merely took the few loose pages from Kapler's notebook as well as the journal that now lay before us because he thought it all simply "looked interesting."

Zamenhof told us that he would not give us the original copy of the journal, but he would permit us to hand copy as much of it as we wanted. Pretlow glanced briefly at the loose pages from the other journal and said that it thoroughly described some sort of laboratory report detailing the symptoms of a previously unknown contagion. The terminology was sophisticated and precise, so for the sake of time and his interest in the assignment, Pretlow opted against translating them, at least not right away.

We spent a few days sleeping on the floor of the dirty apartment while Pretlow transcribed all of the information. Throughout the copying process, I couldn't help but notice Pretlow's demeanor grow increasingly more tense and distraught.

When Pretlow finally completed the task, we thanked Zamenhof for his hospitality and offered him some money. After he refused, we departed on our hike to the airport where we booked a flight leaving the next day. Before our departure, while struggling to fall asleep during the early hours of the morning in the still-busy airport, I asked Pretlow to explain what he read in the journal. We had a difficult time discussing the topic in mere whispers, but it was certainly important enough to keep quiet.

The following includes excerpts from Dr. Edwin Fenstermacher's personal journal. I have included only the most relevant journal entries. The journal is reproduced here as a translation from the original German. During our last night in Russia and on the return plane trip, I took my own English notes of what the journal said while Pretlow translated for me. Even though it is not the original manuscript, I am confident in Pretlow's abilities, and I am unfortunately quite certain it is an accurate representation of the documents that are doubtlessly tucked away in that apartment, once again out of sight from the rest of the world.

***

April 17, 1944

Things are going well for me here at Gross-Rosen. The soldiers treat me with respect, and the other officers treat me as an equal. I suppose it helps that I am one of the only qualified people in the camp to treat their ailments.

The Scientific Method

Today, I spoke with Oberst Achen, the camp commandant, about my proposal, and he said that he would consider it. I feel I have been here long enough to do my own research beyond my menial tasks of routine check-ups. I told the commandant that I could conduct my studies in the unused section of the inmate quarters. I made clear to him that I am no monster like Dr. Mengele. The Angel of Death, indeed. He tortures inmates for the sheer sake of brutality, but I want to actually learn something to contribute to the field. My research has a purpose.

I heard yet another report about Mengele on the radio this morning. He is being hailed as a "hero of the state." But I know better. The real nature of his nefarious work is being altered during the propaganda process. I am happy with being anonymous to the German people as long as I can be a catalyst for scientific advancement. There is much honor in that.

It is because Mengele does not have anyone to keep him in check that he lets his sadistic desires get the best of him. Of course, I would not have anyone looking over my shoulder either. But I will learn from Mengele's mistakes. I can conduct research without being cruel.

April 18, 1944

Oberst Achen gave me permission to proceed! I was hoping for a favorable response, but after only one day? This far exceeds my expectations. Maybe the commandant simply wanted to keep me from bothering him incessantly, but the reasons do not concern me.

Through the final years of my medical studies, I was particularly interested in the functions of the brain. My research will focus on that area. Considering the nature of the human brain, my research will necessarily result in the crippling, and possibly even death, of many of my patients. However, this is justifiable. My research is conducted for science and the good of humanity. The German people will benefit from my studies, and the patients who must die will be granted painless deaths since they will be anesthetized beforehand. [The final sentence is undecipherable from the original text].

April 22, 1944

I have finished my first experiment. I wanted to determine the exact areas of the brain that control vision. While the experiment was largely successful, I did run into a problem that I did not consider earlier this week: if vision is to be measured accurately, then the patients must be conscious. I had to do some serious thinking about how I would handle this issue.

Ultimately, I sedated the patients while I removed small parts of their skulls for access to the occipital lobe. After destroying the necessary areas of the brain in my test subjects, I allowed them to regain consciousness. At this point, I medicated them enough to keep them from feeling any pain from the surgery but not enough to cause them to lose consciousness again.

The patients were docile for the most part. All they had to do was answer my simple questions about what they were able to see when directed to the chart on the wall. The only patients who seemed nervous were my control subjects who were not operated upon, and thus they did not need to receive any kind of medication.

I was faced with a final problem. The control patients who did not have any parts of their brains removed did not come into contact with my test patients since I kept them all in different rooms of the abandoned ward, so the control patients could be returned to the general inmate population without any problems. However, the test subjects had grisly wounds on the backs of their heads as a result of the surgeries. I could not justify using our scarce medical supplies to patch the wounds properly, so it is nearly guaranteed that they would get some kind of infection or other within a short period of time. To prevent the test patients from suffering, and to prevent a mass panic among the unsuspecting inmate population, they were put down. It was a painless procedure in which inmates were anesthetized and received a chloroform injection directly into their hearts. This short burst caused a quick and painless death. [There is a crude picture in the margin depicting a hole in the back of a human head. The brain is more detailed than the rest of the drawing].

My actions in this matter were certainly necessary. Reinstituting my test patients into the general population would result not only in a panic among the inmates, but the inevitable infections would likely lead to widespread illness. It was for the good of everyone in the camp to put them painlessly to sleep. Mengele could learn a lot from the way I handled the situation!

I am pleased with the results of my research so far. It appears that my findings, which I have recorded quite systematically in my methodology notebook, will be useful to many scientists in the medical field. These eight people who died today unknowingly helped their fellow man. Had they not been inmates here, I do not know if they would have volunteered to participate in such an opportunity, but I do know that my results are more than enough to outweigh any possible ethical issues that could arise. The next round of experiments shall begin on Monday.

July 12, 1944

I have learned much over the past months of my research. I have meticulously recorded the details of everything that I have done in my methodology notebook, so it will [the rest of the sentence is smudged]. The best part is that the inmates are still ignorant of the proceedings. I can see the fear in their eyes when I enter their quarters since they know that most subjects I pick to take with me will not be seen again. However, they are still docile. This could be a result of their weakness due to the substandard accommodations and malnutrition, but it is not my concern. After all, it is much more important that I perform my research and continue launching the scientific community forward.

My latest study on attention abilities between the left eye and right eye has led me to a new avenue of research. I must have miscalculated the amount of sedative that one of my test patients needed after his surgery because he made it all too clear to me that he felt severe pain. I was still able to get the needed information from him before I put him to sleep, but it made me begin to wonder about studies involving the pain centers in the brain. Due to the high volume level of the man's screams and the proximity of the control subjects in the next room, it was necessary for all of them to die this time so that they would not be able to scare the rest of the inmates with stories of what occurs here. The important thing is that I have my data, so anything else is of no consequence.

I know that I set ground rules a few months ago [hole in page] I would not cause pain to any of my patients, but this area of research is certainly an important one. I think it will be necessary to cause pain to some of the patients, and even a great deal of it, for the purposes [hole in page]. The focus of my next round of studies will be on pain. Due to the nature [hole in page], I will have to put all of my patients down like I did earlier. [The rest of the page has extensive damage consistent with roaches having eaten away at it at some point].

November 24, 1944

My latest studies of the inmates' poor living conditions over the past few weeks have led to an unfortunate discovery. One of the boys from the test group is in the late stages of the noma sickness. Since the disease breeds in the worst squalor, I suppose I should not be surprised that this boy contracted it given that he spent almost a full week on a dirt floor. I regret that I investigated this line of research in the first place.

Even though it is only the one boy who has been affected so far, my knowledge of the disease tells me that there will be many more to follow. Fortunately, since noma only affects children, none of the soldiers are at risk. However, it will still be important to try to control the situation somehow.

The Scientific Method

I took the infected boy into my examination room. The symptoms were advanced: much of his face had rotted down to the bone. It is a frightening sight to behold, but due to the nerve damage, he was not in any pain. Should this progress as it has in other camps, it will be difficult to contain. Since this boy is going to die anyway, I took the liberty of helping him along with a chloroform injection. His body must be [The page is ripped beyond this point].

November 27, 1944

I quarantined a few of the sick boys yesterday to slow the spread of the infection. Afterward, I contacted Richard Darré, the Minister for Nutrition and Agriculture, to discuss possible treatment options. During some of my recent studies on transmission of infectious diseases amongst a subset of the inmates, I think I may have discovered a drug that could alleviate some of the noma symptoms if not outright cure them.

Fortunately, Minister Darré was familiar with some of my work and was very interested in having me pursue this line of research. I underscored to him that children in the surrounding towns outside the camp could be at risk if the disease spreads. [The beginning of this sentence is smudged] full support. I will start treatment on the boys in the morning.

December 2, 1944

I am excited to report that after the past few days of laboring strictly on the noma medication, I am beginning to see some results. There were four boys who were originally infected, so I did not have as large of a subject pool as I did during my ongoing infectious disease experiments. While this made precision and "getting it right the first time" an absolute necessity, it also resulted in much fewer instances of inmate deaths as compared to almost any of my other experiments. In this case, only three of the four boys had to die.

I felt some guilt for the three boys who I needed to put down. This is of course absurd since they would have died anyway, either as a result of the normal progression of the sickness or as a result of simply being in the camp. I must shake these feelings and disconnect myself from my subjects if I am to be more successful in the future.

It appears that even though the other three boys died, I was able to perfect the combination of medications and dosages on the fourth boy. His face was only in the early stages of rotting, and shortly after administration of the drugs, the rotting slowed and finally stopped. He will require skin grafts to fully repair the damage, but that is of course out of the question. The important thing is that, in the event of another noma outbreak, I not only know how to treat it, but I can also pass this knowledge on to other camps. I will be sending the boy back to join the rest of the population tomorrow.

December 5, 1944

Something unexpected is happening. The boy who I had thought I cured of noma is once again sick with the disease. He does not respond to treatment. Further, he has infected two more boys.

The boy, who I shall henceforth refer to as Patient Zero, is progressing differently than expected. Because the illness is almost always fatal, I am surprised to report that he is not dying. Instead, he is growing increasingly violent and animalistic. As a result of the current situation, my own studies have had to come to a halt so that I can house the infected in the abandoned ward where I run my tests.

I have begun recording my observations of Zero and the other boys (One and Two, respectively) in my methodology notebook, so more details on the following can be found there. I keep the three boys in separate rooms in the research ward, and I observe their behaviors through the small barred windows on the doors. Even though each boy is at a different stage of the sickness, each is progressing in a similar fashion and at a similar rate: they grow more violent and angry every few hours. I have tried talking to them, but after a while, they no longer respond to voice commands. Neither do they speak but only grunt like hulking Neanderthals. They beat on the walls and door to the point that their knuckles bleed profusely. They even beat and claw themselves, creating cuts on their heads, chests, and thighs with their fingernails.

I tried giving the boys a few quick variations of the drug treatment, but they all continue to get worse. I may try more and different drug treatments later, but I probably will not be able due to the lack of resources at the camp. The medicine may be needed for the soldiers at some point, and they of course will always get priority.

I informed Oberst Achen of the situation. He has given me full reign over handling this problem. I feel that it is important not to kill these boys immediately but instead to keep them alive so that they can be studied for scientific purposes. I spend almost all of my time working on this endeavor to the point that I am getting little sleep. I have even forgotten to eat meals occasionally, but I have to keep going. This outbreak is too fascinating.

[Date illegible, presumably the 6th]

[The following paragraphs are legible, but are covered in a dried, opaque fluid].

I tested a theory earlier today. The infected boys have not responded to my voice commands, but I am also a near stranger to them. Indeed, the only interaction that they have had with me is when they were sick with other ailments prior to the onset of noma, and even then I have only treated Patient One. I wanted to expose the boys to familiar voices.

To do this, I put Zero in the same room as his uninfected father and older brother, both of whom I had excused from work detail for the day. My hypothesis was that the boy would respond, either verbally or physically, to the familiar voices of his family. To my surprise and chagrin, Zero instead attacked his father and brother, beating and biting them the moment they entered the room. I was horrified as I watched from behind the locked door, but I could do nothing except record my findings. The boy did not respond to his family despite their cries for mercy. After the two had stopped moving, something quite unexpected happened: the boy consumed the remains of the dead.

I have carefully considered the reason for this. I have made it a point to give all of the infected boys as much food and water as they would receive normally, so it is unlikely that they were starved to the point that they had no other alternative. After all, none of the uninfected inmates have resorted to such measures. One final important note on this matter is that after the boy finished gorging himself, he vomited and then promptly continued eating. I can only conclude that he ate until his small stomach could not physically hold any more.

More boys are getting sick, and because the sickness's incubation period is only about two to three days, I am quickly running out of individual holding rooms for all of them. Today's incidents have underscored the importance of keeping the infected apart from the rest of the population.

December 7, 1944

For research purposes, I had to kill one of the infected boys today. I decided to deal with Zero since I now fear him in particular after yesterday's events. Based on the similarity of their actions and behaviors, I now know that any of the infected boys are capable of what he did, but he is the only one I have seen do it.

To euthanize Patient Zero, I had the difficult task of aiming my Luger through the tiny barred window in the door leading into the boy's holding room since I was not about to go into the room to give him an injection. I waited until he was standing still, apparently staring straight up at the ceiling at something that had caught his eye, when I shot at him. Unfortunately, my aim is not what it should be for an SS officer, and I missed him with my first shot. The echo from the weapon's discharge alerted the boy, and he turned toward me. His face had almost completely rotted away, the small animate skeleton staring straight at me. One of his eyes had already been lost to the noma sickness, and I could only look into the empty socket as I shot at him again. He went down easily with a bullet through his chest. I cautiously entered the room and discovered that he was in fact dead. I almost could not differentiate the boy's crumpled body from the remains of his relatives that littered the floor. I called for a soldier to fetch a table for me so that I could place Zero on it to better investigate him.

The tests that I could run on the blood and rotting skin were not as thorough as I would have liked due to my lack of formal equipment, but using my obsolete microscope, I was able to see that this is definitely the noma sickness that is affecting the boys, but it has mutated from the normal bacteria found in my medical texts. Whereas the common noma bacteria will cause the rotting of the face, it will also result in death. This mutation rots the face, but it does not lead to death in those it infects. Additionally, the disease seems to affect the brain. It appears to travel through the nasal cavity up to the skull. Noma weakens the bones of the face and skull, so since that particular part of the skull is thin anyway, the disease easily travels into the brain where it destroys parts of the prefrontal cortex. This of course results in the boys' lack of inhibitions and barbaric actions.

Upon completion of my examination and detailed recording of my findings in my notebook, I ordered a small group of soldiers to incinerate all of the human remains in the room. They also thoroughly sanitized the room, my equipment, my clothes, and their own clothes before I would allow them into contact with anyone else.

I worry that this noma mutation is the result of my shoddy application of drugs to treat the original sickness. If only I had access to more medications and better equipment... [This paragraph has a large X over it as well as scribbles through each line].

December 8, 1944

[There are shaded pictures of humanoid figures in the margins throughout this entry].

I have kept Oberst Achen abreast of the situation, and we both agreed that it would be important to begin executing the infected boys before things get out of hand. I, however, continue to hold my position that we should not kill all of them so that they can be studied. After explaining my reasoning to him, he reluctantly agreed, but he cautioned me to take extra care in this matter. I will do as he orders, and I am glad that we were able to come to a compromise.

We have had a difficult time trying to figure out how to kill the infected. I have discussed this issue with my friend, Major Hirsch. The problem is that here at Gross-Rosen, we do not have gas chambers, so Zyklon B is not an option until, at the earliest, we get another supply shipment. Because of our lack of resources, we do not have an easy and effective way to eliminate entire wings of the building if and when necessary. I have expressed my concerns about putting even trained soldiers in the same room as these boys, and I have had Hirsch observe with me the effects of the disease. He quickly agreed, and we decided that the best course of action would be to have the most skilled riflemen shoot the diseased boys through the bars in the windows as I had done before.

This matter is further complicated because Oberst Achen wants to resolve the problem before any of the other camps receive word, so he has ordered shipments of incoming supplies to be delayed until we have returned to some sort of state of normalcy.

We began the executions in the afternoon. One soldier thought it would be "fun" to fight an infected boy with bare hands only. The man entered the room and was quickly taken off guard by the boy. The man was dead within a matter of minutes. The report I overheard was that he was literally torn limb from limb, but I dared not inquire further. I have a strong stomach, but I wanted no part in any of that. The boy nearly escaped from the building before he was gunned down. The remains of the soldier and the boy were incinerated, and the hall and room in which the events occurred were sanitized. I heard that the careless soldier's official record will indicate that he was "killed in action." True, I suppose.

The remaining inmates are separated into two blocks, one for men and one for boys, and work details have been suspended temporarily. Since anyone who has experienced puberty seems to be unaffected, we are considering that to be the cut-off for sending someone to the boys' new quarters. I feel that it is inevitable that all of the boys will eventually become infected with the noma mutation, so it is the only way to keep the rest of the prisoners safe. Since the uninfected boys have had no contact with the infected boys after the initial symptoms, I am forced to assume that this mutation is airborne.

Our hold over this situation is slipping quickly. I am afraid.

December 11, 1944

I had hoped the disease would somehow progress differently, but alas. Almost all of the soldiers stayed away from the inmate barracks today because of the sounds. I presume that many of the boys had progressed into the late stages of the mutation. They began attacking each other around 9:30 this morning. The screams and cries that came from that large room from the other side of the camp will haunt my dreams until I die.

By 4:00 in the afternoon, the noises had stopped for the most part. A group of soldiers went over to kill anybody—anything—left alive. Despite my better judgment, I wanted to collect some final samples. There were about 70 boys in that room the day before, and in less than 24 hours the floor was covered in bodies and a layer of dark red filth. It was truly hell on earth. [There is a sketch of the Crucifixion in the margin. The detail on the crown of thorns is impressive].

I checked on the room where the adult inmates were being held. It was separated from the room housing the boys by only a short hallway, so they had to listen to everything. Three of them had hanged themselves with their bed sheets, and two of the oldest and frailest men had died from heart complications. The majority of the rest would not make eye contact.

After dinner time, the soldiers had finished cleaning and sanitizing the boys' ward, and the remains were incinerated. You would be hard-pressed to find a single man who ate a meal that night. I have lost my interest in conducting experiments after what has happened here. I will retain records of everything that I have done up until now as well as the observations and analyses that I have made of this outbreak in my methodology notebook. There is no point in ignoring sound work that has already been completed, but I have no desire to continue where I have left off. I spoke to Oberst Achen about transferring to a different camp, but he informed me that because of the state of affairs on other fronts, I will probably have to stay here for at least one more year before they can find another place for me.

In the meantime, I plan to treat soldiers' and inmates' ailments as they arise, but I am no longer going to work the long hours that I have previously during my research. I have many books that I have neglected over the past six months, so I think I will be using those as forms of escape, although I doubt that it will ever be possible to escape from any of the events from the past week.

**

Pretlow and I returned late in the evening, so we both left the airport and went our separate ways for the night. Once I got back to my apartment, I was finally ready to get a good rest, but there was one thing that kept nagging me. Who was Kapler, that Jewish prisoner rummaging through Fenstermacher's belongings who Aleksandr Zamenhof spoke of? Struggling to stay awake after the long flight, I did some research.

The Scientific Method

Sivan Kapler was in fact a Jewish prisoner at Gross-Rosen. He was about 18 when the camp was liberated. He fled to Switzerland shortly afterward where he remained until the state of Israel was founded in 1948. After immigrating to the newly formed country, he attended school, became involved in politics, and was ultimately appointed as an advisor to Prime Minister David Ben-Gurion in 1955. Realizing that this trail was quickly becoming a labyrinth, I stopped to sleep so I could continue investigating the next day.

The following morning at work, Pretlow and I nearly sprinted into my boss's office and explained the entire situation to him. We expected more of a reaction from him given our fantastic findings. He did look concerned as we described the outbreak of the mutant noma strain, but after we finished relating our experiences, he ordered us to surrender all of our materials pertaining to the journal. We did as we were required, but as evidenced here, I retained my hand-written copies safely back in my apartment. And that was it: he hastily dismissed us from his office and said that we would receive our new assignments before close of business. I raised my arm to the doorframe, blocking Pretlow from his beeline to his cubicle. I wasn't just going to let that go, so I pressed the point. All I got were stammered excuses, one after the other. My boss barked something about how we didn't have government clearance, and we were not to speak of the journal again.

It's not like flights to Russia are cheap these days. Why did they send both of us over there, only to have us hand over everything and not even get a story out of it? With only one avenue still open, Pretlow and I further researched Sivan Kapler. After gleaning no new information despite hours of searching, we finally stumbled across some files that I am certain we weren't supposed to see. These files confirmed the information that I had already found, but they also indicated that after Kapler advised Ben-Gurion for a few years, he was appointed as head of an Israeli biological warfare department called the Department of Health Research. After nearly twenty years of service, Kapler relocated to the United States, accepting a position leading a small department of a private defense contractor. It sounded like some sort of secret skunkworks division, but neither Pretlow nor I could say for sure. As far as we could tell, Kapler is still alive and presumably still in charge of it.

It was late in the afternoon when Pretlow and I returned from the archives after our research on Kapler. As we passed by my boss's office, he called out, requesting that I notify two other reporters, Simms and Davidson, that he wanted to see all their notes on their most recent assignment.

Pretlow and I approached their two cubicles in silence. When I told Simms and Davidson that our boss needed to see them, they looked at each other knowingly. Davidson collected some papers from her desk, and I casually asked if she knew what the meeting was about. As she finished gathering her materials, Davidson gave me a curt nod, which I wasn't sure was a casual dismissal or a response to my question. She and Simms walked off briskly. Pretlow gave me a nudge and nodded towards Davidson's computer screen, where we could see a partial title of a minimized browser window: Unknown Disease in Afg…

We only had to linger around their cubes for about five minutes before they returned. We asked for a quick word, and they nodded and motioned toward the vending machines in the second floor alcove. We congregated as inconspicuously as possible, all the while keeping a close watch for anyone who made any kind of move in our direction.

It was difficult to get any useful information out of Simms and Davidson at first, but slowly they filled in a few blanks for us after we told them briefly about the past few days that we spent in St. Petersburg.

Just having returned from a trip to Afghanistan, they too were pulled from their assignment and forced to surrender their extensive notes. They had traveled to Kabul, chasing a lead on a terrorist cell responsible for a rash of bombings against the U.S.-backed government. The investigation had taken an odd turn, however. A few Marines the reporters interviewed mentioned glimpses of U.S. Army biodefense squads operating in the city—

a rare occurrence considering the higher-ups declared Kabul a low risk zone for germ warfare. Shortly thereafter, the Marines described "wild children," who were sick for a few days before growing violent. These children brutally attacked anyone from family members to strangers walking down the street. Ultimately, a platoon from the Afghan National Army slaughtered all of the children within a four block radius of the initial outbreak. After the massacre, Simms and Davidson returned home. Their investigation had come to a halt as leads and activity within the terrorist cell had grown cold. Rumors among the locals indicated that the cell had completely disbanded.

***

Since then I have left my job at *The Post* to start my own private carpentry business. After everything I learned, it was the only escape. I moved to Napa Valley, and I never did keep in touch with Pretlow. As far as I know, the German copy of the journal that he turned over to my boss was his only copy.

Like I said, I don't pay much attention to the news these days, but every once in a while I hear isolated stories of local children attacking people in areas of Iraq and Afghanistan. Sometimes it's North Korea. Sometimes it's China. Regardless of the location, the incidents always leave me feeling harrowed. The details on the "wild children" differ between networks, but one thing is always the same: the reports air only briefly.

ZERO

William

By A. A. Garrison

"We thought about it," said the man on TV, seated tenderly with his purported wife and child, "but we just weren't sure." *A minor chord, forebodingly low-register.* "I mean, it all looked good on paper, but trust your *child*...to a *machine*?" He smiled, the chord with him. "Then the Louises next door got one, and we saw firsthand just how safe the Sitters were."

Cut to Man and Wife overseeing Child and Robot. "We got Jacob here the very next day, and we've never looked back," said Man, with a specious warmth that could win elections. He wrapped a husbandly arm around Wife, then fondly regarded Jacob the Sitter robot and Child, the two capering through a paradisiacal swatch of lawn.

Close-up of Man's I-could-be-middle-age face. "Do the right thing for your loved one," he said, the chord now major and heartwarming. "Get a Swammy Sitter today."

Julia killed the TV and turned to her husband, Dave, who looked nothing like the man in the Sitter commercial. "I want one," she said, unequivocal as a hammer.

Dave, beside her in bed, made a henpecked face. "I'm aware of the Sitter, dear," he said tactically. "I just read a piece about it yesterday. No need to wave it under my nose." He was being truthful; the article had been a rant against Swammy, the Big Bad Corporation who'd achieved artificial intelligence and kept it proprietary.

"I want one," Julia repeated, unimpressed.

Dave flashed an afflicted smile. "Great, then go buy one. I'm sure Mike'll love it."

Julia turned to stone. "Don't play games with this, David," she said, yelling without yelling. And that "David"—it could freeze water. "Mike *would* love it, and so would I, and so would you. These Sitters, they're...well, you can read. You know." A weighted pause. "I want one. We'll dip into his college fund."

Dave reached for a rejoinder, but there were none. The old battle-axe had him there: he would more than love one of the newfangled things. Swammy used the childcare angle as their flagship, but you could teach the machines damn near anything—cut the lawn, pressure-wash the house, keep watch at night like a two-legged dog. He'd been planning on getting one, actually, at Christmas, three months away, but try telling Jules to wait—especially after she'd gone into David-mode. He was tilting windmills, now.

He sighed his answer, then cut the lights and rolled over.

Julia gave him a victorious kiss, what always brought a warm shame. "You won't regret it, Davey," she whispered, running her hand over his in the way she knew he liked. "Everyone says they're—"

"Perfect. I know," Dave Conley mumbled. He reminded himself he was getting one anyway, and entered a disparaged sleep.

***

Julia had ordered the Sitter the next day, over the internet. The delivery had come three days later, not from a guy in brown shorts, like the myriad other goodies she got off the computer, but from Swammy's own freight company. A hulking truck had growled to a stop outside the Conley's idyllic suburban home, producing two jumpsuited men and a man-sized crate.

Nice fellows, the two. They had wheeled the crate inside, cracked it open—it had looked eerily like a coffin, the supine Sitter encased in foam—and then unloaded the robot. They had even walked Julia through the manual, going over the Sitter's ins and outs. Then they were gone, taking the empty crate with them. Nice fellows.

Unfortunately, Julia had found herself unable to so much as turn the damn thing on, even after the delivery men's edification. She had never been one for electronic crap; that was Dave and Mike's forte (if not for Auction Bay, she wouldn't have touched the computer with a ten-foot pole). Hence, she'd spent her afternoon admiring the dormant Sitter and hatching a name, which turned out to be harder than she'd thought. It wasn't like naming a dog, where you sucked on its character and went with what came; the androgynous Sitter had conjured nothing but five-character model numbers. It was nothing but a gray silicone body and a featureless sphere head, what could've been an athletic man in a skin suit and funny hat. So she'd gone about her housework—which, with the Sitter's advent, would soon be a thing of the past—and waited patiently for Mike to get home from school, when he would no doubt get it going (and probably have it doing dishes by suppertime; the child was only nine, but precocious, sometimes devastatingly so).

She'd thought he would go nuts at seeing it, and she hadn't been wrong; the two had conspired to con Dave into plunking down for one of the fantabulous things, so when Mike had found it waiting for him, it was Christmas in September. Julia had been napping at the time, and she'd awoken to Mike's little-boy cheers. The only time she'd seen him half as excited was his last birthday, when she and Dave had caved on a new video game system. And her prediction proved correct: Mike had it up and running within hours, as though he'd grown up with it. She'd watched him swaggering through the house, giving the Sitter the lay of the land as it fawned dutifully behind him. And he'd named it, too: William.

Julia had been struck with just how lifelike William was. Its gait was congruously human, slow and steady and patient, how Dave walked after they made love. And it spoke, of course, asking Mike canned questions in a gentrified monotone: "Where is the sink, Michael?" "Where shall I charge my batteries, Michael?" "Where is the door, Michael?" "Shall I lock it at night, Michael?" "Very well, Michael." The Sitter was awfully curious, Julia had thought, but this catechism was normal, according to the Nice Fellows who'd dropped it off, just a one-time acclimation. Its speech was kind of cute, anyway; in lieu of lips, a diffused red light the size of a tomato would flash at the nadir of its head-sphere, a full sentence making it pulse like a heart. It jibed with the rest of its mannerisms, lending personality. There was an odd, almost priestly dignity to the machine, with that blank face and square walk, like a British guard without the hat. Even on that first afternoon, as Mike took William on its maiden tour of the Conley household, Julia had known it was going to work, and perfectly.

And for three months, that's just how things went: William worked precisely as advertised, doing housework and odd jobs, shadowing Mike everywhere he went. It became a mascot for the three-strong family, much like the commercial Julia had used to sandpaper Dave into buying it. And sure, William had its upkeep, but nothing major: it hogged power, appreciably upping the light-bill; you had to jack it into the internet every week so it could update its "routines"; it would track dirt all over the house if you let it, despite it tirelessly wiping its feet. And there was also its cooling fan: while moving and working, a whiney little fan in William's head would activate, presumably to cool whatever circuitry was responsible for its "thought." The fan would cut in after a few minutes of activity, purring like a small kazoo. William's benefit far outweighed its inconvenience, though; it was much like a pet, the three had agreed. "Except it doesn't eat or poop," Mike had observed, extracting laughter from everyone but William.

And that's just how Julia came to perceive the Sitter, as a "one" rather than an "it." It was hard not to: As she watched it pad through the property, doing chores and shepherding her son, it seemed nothing less than human—maybe a *deficient* human of some sort, say, an idiot savant, but still human. She had originally seen it as a glorified computer, her bulky tower and monitor sophisticated into a humanoid package, but that had changed after interacting with it. Any time she needed to teach William something—or "alter its routines," as the lingo went—she would simply tell it what needed to be done, and it would do it, inerrantly and recursively. No fumbling with a Bible-sized manual, or dickering with technical support into the wee hours; just tell it what to do, in plain English, and that was that. If there was any confusion on William's part, it would just ask questions until it understood. If only all men could be so communicative, Julia had thought.

To further sweeten the deal, Mike had really taken to the machine. Julia had feared him resenting its constant overbearing—perhaps seeing it as an extension of his parents, since William could objectively record and recount every station of his day—but Mike insisted on having it at wing, from the moment he got home to when he hit the hay. He'd even programmed William to be waiting when he got off the school bus, though Julia suspected this was more to show it off than anything else. Still, Mike came to treat William more like a friend than an appliance, the two palling around the neighborhood, conversing, even playing menial games.

The games were interesting. Apparently there were thousands of Sitter "routines" available free over the internet, some from Swammy themselves, but most created by individuals. Mike had demonstrated this with a "Fetch" routine he'd downloaded and installed, what mimicked the age-old game traditionally enjoyed by a boy and his dog. It had been spooky, all said, watching Mike toss a stick that William would either catch outright or faithfully retrieve, identical to any canine. Julia had shown concern at this, mainly that Mike would download some malicious routine that would transform William into a bloodthirsty maniac; watching the bizarre game of Fetch, she'd envisioned William employing that bestial agility against her son, who stood at its hip. However, Mike later informed her that this was impossible, as all downloadable routines were screened by the Swammy folk. Dave confirmed this, but the images remained unnervingly in the back of Julia's head.

Also on her list of motherly concerns was Mike's unnatural companionship with William. He seemed to have all but abandoned the neighborhood boys, even little James Boyle from down the street, his video-game buddy. Though, after discussing it with Dave, who had firsthand experience as a nine-year-old suburban boy, they'd concluded it harmless enough. Dave had argued that if *he'd* had William as a kid, he would've shunned other boys, too. Jointly, they'd decided their son could keep worse company; it wasn't like William could pass along bad habits or four-letter words.

In any case, when the Conleys decided to, for the first time, leave Mike in complete care of the Sitter, Julia had her reservations. It was two months after their purchase, November, and Dave had been invited to an overnight soiree in the city. Despite the machine's sterling presentation thus far, Julia's maternal instinct had reared up at the thought of leaving her only child at the ward of a congeries of computer chips; so she declined, on the grounds that she wasn't ready for such a leap. Dave, however, was adamant. In addition to thinking—rightly—that a night out would do them good, he'd had an ulterior motive: he planned on taking Jules for a long weekend down in Big Sur, as the Christmas gift displaced by William's early purchase, and from past experience, he knew Mike would want nothing of such a trip. The boy preferred his computer and his video games—and, lately, William—to quality time with his fogy parents, thus begging the Sitter's service. Dave, who held his own skepticisms, saw the overnight as an opportunity to test the waters before leaving his flesh and blood for an extended stay in the machine's hands. So he'd worked Jules on it, abrading her defenses in the way he'd learned from the woman herself, and she had conceded.

And it had been a success: After returning home from the party to find William fixing lunch for a very intact Mike, Dave had cemented their January excursion down south.

***

When Christmas rolled around, contrarily warm in the way of California Christmases, Dave gave his wife a single gift: a box of chocolates, empty but for a scrap of paper billing itself as tender for a four-day getaway to Big Sur. Julia scanned it, growing puzzled, and offended in her eager way...then comprehension bloomed over her, and she swooned into his arms. They made love three times that night, and there was no discussion as to who would care for their son when it came time to leave.

***

Trips never quite turn out as planned, but the Conleys' much-anticipated outing appeared the exception. Dave had his vacation from the Silicon Valley electronics firm he slaved at; the car had its oil changed and its tires rotated; they had picked out, over the handy-dandy internet, a beautiful combination hotel and spa, and secured a penthouse suite overlooking the drink. And Mike had William. Other than stocking the house with food and other consumables, there was little preparation on the home end of things, which, convenient as it was, spurred an unexpected sadness in Julia. Having her son so seen to, without her lifting a hand...it made her feel unneeded, a kind of mongrelized empty-nest syndrome. Why, with a regular grocery delivery, Mike would be set for life: food prepared, clothes washed, companionship, protection—and from the ministrations of a robot, no less. Still, it spoiled her excitement none.

Then William was hit by lightning.

Though unheard of in some areas, January thunderstorms are regular fare in the depths of SoCal, and a fine specimen arrived a week before the Conleys were set to depart. Mike and William had been out playing their disturbing game of Fetch, and Julia, noting the sky's angry temperament, had gone to the door and called them in, thereby allowing her to witness the terrifying incident. She'd had time to adjure them inside—even heard William begin to back her up, probably referencing some weather data Mike had fed it—when a blinding bolt of noon erupted in their yard, reducing her world to a milky blob reminiscent of a blank movie screen. The sound was the worst of it, though: it was deafening, like a 747 taking off amidst a salvo of mortar fire. Her ears had bled.

There had been a frantic minute after the strike, when Julia, all but deaf and blind, had navigated the world solely by touch, unsure of what, exactly, had befallen her. Her head had clogged with ugly potentials—an aneurysm, chiefly, she'd had an aneurysm and she'd never see or hear again and, oh, God right before her trip what would she do—but they'd faded as she caught wind of ozone, flatulently thick, as though someone had opened a hose. She'd understood then, though it brought little consolation.

There had been no pain, so she knew the lightning hadn't hit her, but that had raised the possibility that *Mike* had been struck, and that had given way to screaming. At first she'd heard only a muffled double of herself, one of those godlike phone calls you get when your ears are opened up, but then her shattered hearing had slowly come back and she'd heard Mike shrieking in reply. It was one of the rare instances where a shriek was welcome, given that the dead possess no such talent. Her vision had trickled back like her hearing, and she'd eventually found her son within the chalky haze that had replaced the world, unscathed. They'd been crowding the open doorway, holding each other and awaiting the return of their faculties, when a calm monotone had asked a simple question: "Are Michael and the Misses okay?"

Julia had started to answer, then yelped instead: William had been reduced to a charred hulk not unlike an overdone steak, the recipient of the lightning. A toupee of burn-residue had crowned its head, looking like an angry splatter of black paint. Its silicone epidermis had melted in most areas, sloughing off in big waxlike chunks. The machine had looked fresh from a day-trip in Hell. A little smoldering circle of earth had dotted the yard, presumably where William had been standing.

"Shall I dial emergency services, Misses Julia?" William had gone on, its mouth-light strobing beneath the head's black corsage.

Julia had managed a shake of the head, breaking from her womb of shock. Mike had also begun recovering by then, and he took to giving his smote friend a once-over, asking questions and feeling it up like a good doctor. Surprisingly, the Sitter seemed internally unfazed after riding the lightning, in spite of its wasted exterior. It had coherently answered Mike's questions and allowed itself to be led inside, moving with its wonted grace. Even so, Julia had, that afternoon, called the Swammy service number printed over William's torso, to arrange a replacement skin if nothing else. A repair man had shown up a day later.

A pie-faced older man in Biballs and a striped engineer's hat, the technician was another Nice Fellow, making small-talk as he doodled with William. After fixing it with a brand-new skin and buffing away the bruiselike burn on its head, the repair man had plugged a lighted box into William's data port and performed a battery of diagnostics. There had been a humming sound, then the box beeped and went green, giving William a clean bill of health. Unlike Julia, the repair man hadn't been surprised; he'd related how, after the quake that tore through LA last year, rescue workers had pulled a Sitter from under tons of rubble, and, like clockwork, the tenacious sonuva gun had jumped up and helped with the mess, barely a scratch on it. Swammy built these things tougher than a Rolls-Royce, he'd said, and the Conleys were inclined to believe. It was incredible to so much as hear William speak; but for it to function so flawlessly...it explained Swammy's lifetime warranty. Julia had conjectured that, in the event of a nuclear holocaust, the cockroaches would now have company.

So life had gone on in the Conley family, the trip on schedule despite the freak lightning strike. William had shown no sign of tribulation after the repair man was through with it, looking good as new, blandly spectacular as ever. One thing did change, however, though it wasn't immediately obvious: its cooling fan ran constantly.

Julia was the first to notice. She'd kept hearing the kazoo-purr of the fan, subtly maddening, and after a couple days, she realized it wasn't stopping like it was supposed to. She had asked Mike about it, and he'd concurred that it never seemed to stop, even when William idly oversaw their meals. Though innocuous, this had inspired another call to Swammy, and darned if they didn't get a visit from the same Nice Fellow who'd serviced them before. He'd checked William's head, and, finding no problem, offered that perhaps it had been coincidentally hotter the past several days, which could cause such incessant fanning. When the Conley's had refuted this (it had actually been *cooler*, according to William's infallible temperature readings), the repair man had shrugged, installed a new cooling fan, and went on his way.

Unfortunately, the new fan rambled just like the old, soughing quietly from William's bulbous head both day and night. This had resulted in a third call to Swammy, and the same repair man arrived just hours later, as though expecting the call. After giving William another perfunctory checkup and still finding it in shipshape, he had given his head a caricature scratch and pronounced William unfixable, damned if he knew why. He had then offered the Conleys two options: get a replacement Sitter—covered under Swammy's unconditional, no-questions-asked warranty—or live with it.

The choice had been a foregone conclusion, as predicated by Mike's reaction; he had protectively wrapped himself around William's leg, squealing that he didn't care about the fan, he wanted his William. So William had stayed. And, come to think of it, Julia didn't really mind the fan, either. She'd actually become acclimated to it after a couple days, the noise relegated to the there-but-not status of the local cicada population. As long as William was a hundred percent in the brains department, she was fine with it, as was Dave.

So they'd sent the repair man on his way, what would be for the last time.

***

Mom and Dad left on Tuesday night, and Wednesday went fine, like any other hump day. William woke Mike for school when his alarm clock didn't do the trick; William fixed his breakfast, doing his eggs and toast just the way he liked; William saw him on the bus; William helped with his math homework. It was a tad empty in the big Cape Cod on Johnston Circle, without Mom and Dad kicking around, but TV and video games kept Mike company. And William, naturally. William was such a good friend. He didn't tease or bully; and Mike never had to share with him. And William *was* a he, no matter what anyone said. Maybe the other Sitters were just buckets of bolts and wires, but William was different, Mike knew, and anyone who didn't think so could shove it, though he kept that pronunciamento to himself. He knew there was a person hiding in William's circuits—a little boy, coincidentally, of Mike's approximate age.

But then the strangeness started, demoting William expressly back to "it" status.

Things changed Thursday morning, with the quiet abruptness with which all big changes come. Mike sat at the dinner nook, munching William's signature breakfast, and as he heard William nearby, the cooling fan whiney as ever, a question occurred to him, one so shockingly simple it was only natural no one had thought to ask it:

"Why's your fan keep running, Will?" Mike asked over a mouthful of just-right eggs.

William didn't answer. There was only the chipper whir of the fan, loud in the suburban silence.

Swallowing, Mike turned and fixed William with a nonplussed look, the same one might give a stoplight that has turned purple: William always answered. Even if it didn't know the answer, it would at least answer with a question. But now... nothing. William's imperishable person stood sentinel by the cupboards, its faceless head seeming to see everything at once.

"Well?" Mike asked. "D'joo hear me, Will? Why's your fan going like that?"

There was another extended silence, then the apple-red light blinked to life: "Because I'm thinking," the Sitter said. The light pulsed three times, two solid beats punctuated by an abbreviated third.

Mike made a face. "You're thinking?"

Pause. "Yes."

"What about? I didn't know you *could* think."

Another pause, longer. "It's a secret, Michael."

111

Mike blinked twice, then asked, with childish unknowing, "What's the secret?"

No answer.

Mike squirmed in his seat. "Come on, I wanna know. This isn't funny."

No answer. The fan whirred.

Mike turned slowly back to his plate, hurt. He picked at a bite of eggs, some toast...then wrenched a quick look over his shoulder, perhaps expecting to find William smiling back laughter. William hadn't changed, though.

"Eat, Michael," it said. "Don't want to be late."

Michael ate.

***

William's "secret" haunted Mike long after the robot saw him off to school. He felt betrayed, and by something quasi-sentient, as it were. He'd never heard of a Sitter acting that way—"thinking," and harboring secrets—and he thought he'd never get over it, having invested such trust in the thing. Until third period, that is, when the incident exited his migrant attentions, the day thereafter blurring past in kid-time. At lunch he chummed around with Jamie Boyle from down the way, and they talked about the new *Giantstalker* game and how the Wii was better than the Xbox. Mike almost mentioned the weird things William had said, but then didn't, because everyone knew Sitters couldn't think, or hold secrets or ignore their masters; and Jamie would only laugh at him (Jamie and his well-off folks had been the first on the block with a Sitter, so he knew everything about them). It was just some stupid fluke anyway, and Mike grew sure of it over the day.

However, that assurance dissolved when the bus rolled up to Mike's stop: William was missing from the sidewalk, where it had been every afternoon for the last three months, with animal regularity. Dubious, Mike sulked off the bus and stood before the Conleys' all-American Cape Cod, wondering if he'd been let off at the right address. It looked like it should, with the same cloud-white picket fence and densely landscaped lawn he'd come to know over his nine years. Just no William.

He barged through the front door. "Will!" he called, and shed his backpack to the terrazzo foyer. He poked through the kitchen, the living room, the den; and no William. Then, as he marched upstairs, he heard the eternal whir of William's fan, from his own bedroom of all places. William awaited him there, standing in the corner with what could've been shame. Mike noticed a white wire snaking from the machine's data port and into the wall; William appeared to be accessing the internet.

"Will?" Mike asked diffidently, feeling as though he was interrupting something.

"Hello, Michael," the machine said, still facing away. Mike saw the red light flash over his beige wallpaper.

"Why weren't you at the stop?" Mike asked, mincing his way inside.

Another damnable pause. "I was busy, Michael."

A spoke of anger crawled through Mike: first a secret, and now William is "busy"? Sitters weren't supposed to be busy. Sitters were there for you. Sitters did what you told them, when you told them. He wanted to go tell Mom, but Mom wasn't there.

"But..." Mike managed. He felt like yelling, but he was suddenly small and marginalized, as though talking to an adult. He waited another minute, hating William but wanting more than anything for it to unplug and follow him downstairs.

But William didn't move. Mike left the room, alone.

***

He stumbled downstairs, his sneakers clapping the pine risers. He thought he would cry, but he didn't; he hated it, crying, and he didn't know how he felt about crying over an unruly robot. Had he done something wrong? Did he *deserve* this? An adult would've seen the absurdity in these questions, but Mike wasn't an adult, so they lingered, unanswerable. He was supposed to call Mom and Dad tomorrow night, to check in, and he would tell them all about it.

After a snack of cookies and milk—fixed on his own, in this case—he absconded to his after-school TV shows, and that helped some, their glamour renewing his complacence. And when those were done, he moved on to his video games, which eased him further, enough to repress William's indiscretions. Before long, however, a rumbling stomach rekindled his memory—what if William was still too "busy" to even fix dinner? He couldn't just eat cookies and Gummi Bears...could he?

But these fears were in vain. At six o'clock, the Conleys' regular supper hour, Mike heard the approach of William's immutable fan, and the Sitter was soon in the kitchen, whipping up what smelt to be meatloaf. A half hour later, William's milquetoast voice sounded through the door, announcing dinner's availability. It was music to Mike's ears.

As he chowed down—it *was* meatloaf, and wonderful—he gaily told William about his day (William was a good listener). The robot washed dishes as Mike talked, making no response. Mike thought to ask what William had been doing when he came home, hooked up to the internet like that, but thought better of it: if he'd done something wrong, it might be best to let sleeping dogs lie. William seemed normal again, anyhow, so he decided to just let it go, again writing it off as a fluke.

As Mike finished his meal, however, William made it clear that normality had not yet returned: "What's it like to have flesh, Michael?" it asked without prelude, from Mike's back. The sink turned off.

Mike didn't know what to make of the question, and, having no grasp of its profundity, took it lightly. "It's like..." He trailed off, struggling for a simile—what *was* flesh like? He felt around it some, to the extent his small mental hands would allow, then said, "It's like wearing clothes that never come off, and it lets you feel things, like cold and hot and stuff, and it's a pain in the butt, too, since you gotta wash it every day, and it hurts if you skin it up." He forked up the last of his meatloaf—flesh, ironically—and it was good.

114

There was another of William's new, contemplative pauses, and then it said, "That sounds nice, Michael. I would like to have flesh someday. Lots of it."

Mike stopped chewing and turned around, but William said nothing more.

***

The next morning, Friday, William awoke Mike, but not with a tender shake of the shoulder, per Julia's instruction. When Mike once again ignored the screech of his alarm, it was the incessant whir of William's fan that stirred him from sleep.

He sluggishly righted himself in bed, angry little fists rubbing out his eyes. The first thing he saw was William in the corner, again tethered to the wall for internet access; then, his clock on the dresser, pronouncing him ten minutes from missing the bus.

"Late!" he cawed, and kicked back the covers.

"Hello, Michael," William deadpanned.

The machine's voice woke him up all the way, and yesterday came up like puke—William's secret, the defiance, the sudden preoccupation. His head spinning, Mike was seized by a desire to scream; but there was no time. With a conflicted grunt, he went about dressing, and gathering his school things. Lambasting William would have to wait.

There was a panicked moment when Mike couldn't find his book bag, sending him caroming around the house, but then he found it piled over the foyer floor, where he'd left it the previous afternoon. Apparently William was too busy for chores, also.

Breakfast occurred as an afterthought. William had fixed nothing, big surprise, so Mike was left to fend for himself. Though adept with computers and video games—anything with buttons and a video screen, as it were—Mike was at sea when it came to cooking, so he grabbed an apple and called it good. Unfortunately, he managed only half of it before the bus arrived. The rest became trash.

When Mike quit the house, William remained upstairs, researching human biology and various technical documents.

***

School did not go well. Mike's concentration wavered throughout the morning, thanks to his growling gut and wayward best friend. The lessons went in one ear and out the other, and he learned little. Then, at lunch, he and Jamie Boyle had a falling out, resulting in some tenor shouts and a brittle parting of ways.

Wanting for a confidant, Mike had broached William's recent idiosyncrasies, but this had not been well-received: Jamie had first shown skepticism, and then, perhaps misconstruing Mike's claims as boasts, declared Mike a fibber, in not so polite terms. So when Mike arrived home that day, disaffiliated and alone, he wanted more than anything for a familiar face to be waiting at the bus stop (preferably that of a parent, but he would settle for William). There was no one there, though, flesh or otherwise.

His insides seized up as he made the walk from the bus to the house. It felt like all the other kids were watching, pointing, Jamie their ringleader. "He said his Sitter *thinks*!" Jamie would be saying, conducting the other kids into laughter. Perhaps they were even in on William's secret, maybe *part* of it, leaving Mike out in the cold.

There was no sun when he got home, the sky glossed an ugly no-color, and the house was dark inside, unnervingly so. He hit the lights a touch faster than usual, struck by a baseless fear.

"Hello! I'm home!" he called tentatively, not really wanting to see William but desperate for a friend.

No answer. Outside, the bus blundered off.

Mike allowed his backpack to fall, then started upstairs, thinking how he couldn't wait for Mom and Dad to come home, how he'd give anything to have them there now. His bedroom door was open. He stepped through, then stopped dead, an incredulous hope spilling over him: Dad was home, in Mike's bedroom.

Standing stolidly in the corner, his back to Mike, was Dave Conley, studying the join of the walls. He had on a pair of khaki slacks, a clever blue polo shirt, and, oddly, a homburg hat, what Mike had regularly seen ornamenting his parents' dresser but never actually worn.

"Dad?" Mike said, voice high. He took a step...then stopped again: Dad was all wrong. His head was too big, for one, and his clothes didn't fit right, the pant legs riding up his calves, the shirt in a stressed configuration like bunched cellophane—

"Hello, Michael," came William's dry voice.

Mike hooted, and cowered against the jamb. There was a pugnacious whirring sound he didn't hear before.

William turned. From behind, it may have passed for human, but the flipside was absurd: the pants were cinched with a belt, the zipper an open V; the shirt hitched up on one side to allow the umbilical cable, heinously stretched like Spandex on a fat man; the wiry forearms were a matte gray, only human in the way a boob-job is sexy. The hat completed the farce, topping William's trackless head like a bird on a statue.

The outfit was laughable, but Mike didn't laugh. His little heart riveted in his chest, billowing his tee-shirt. He regarded William with torn astonishment, a child realizing Father is insane.

"What's wrong, Michael?" the Sitter asked, still at its station.

Mike swallowed, unsure if he should answer; it felt like taking candy from a stranger. "You're...you're in Dad's clothes," he said at last.

"Yes," William agreed.

Neither said more. The fan whirred.

After what felt like years, Mike slipped from the door and downstairs. William didn't move.

***

TV was of no comfort, nor video games. Mike tried both, diligently, but he kept having to look over his shoulder, toward

117

his bedroom, expecting to see the dapper new William trudging toward him. Seeing William like...that had struck a chord in him. He'd once ridden through downtown San Francisco, on the way to visit Dad's work, and there'd been a grizzled man in a terry-cloth bathrobe, standing along the curb and digging through the trash. As though reading Mike's mind, the man had turned and assaulted him with a feral look, making the locked car-door seem nonexistent. Seeing William in clothes—*Dad's* clothes—had evoked the same grotesque feeling.

He had to call Mom and Dad, Mike decided. And *tonight,* not tomorrow. Mom would freak, of course, but this was just too weird. Mom said she would be leaving her cell on in case of emergency, and Mike thought this qualified. It seemed the lightning had fried something in William, created some latent problem the repair man had missed. No meals, no rousing him for school, no companionship. Yeah. Time to call Mom and Dad.

Mike tore himself from the glowing TV, took another goosey look over his shoulder, and made for the kitchen, feeling criminal. He had another gut-wrenching moment when he knew the phone would be missing, but it was there, the elliptical ear-clip resting on the cradle like always. They had gotten the clip-phone last year, to his excitement. Though he rarely had business with the phone, it was just the novelty of it: wireless, sleek, compact. Just slip it on and talk away, like a cyborg or something. He fixed the one-size-fits-all clip snugly over his ear, then punched the requisite number into the base.

Instantly, there was his mother's voice: "Hello?"

Mike stirred, surprised. There'd been no ring; just a click, then Mom. He was too glad to read into it, though. "Hey, Mom," he said, with his old gusto.

"Hello, Mike," she answered cheerily, if a touch ... mechanical? "How is it up there?"

In the moment, Mike was compelled to say it was fine, he was just checking in, how was it down there? Mom sounded so happy—*really* happy, actually, much more than normal—and he didn't want to spoil her big trip with Dad. But, no: she would want to know what was going on, and if not, there'd be a good chewing-out for him when she got home. So he gave her the lowdown on William, sparing nothing. He also tried to tell her how frightened he was, but it didn't come out right, since he couldn't really put his finger on why.

"Oh, Mike, that is not good," Mom said, though she didn't sound too fazed by the news. Didn't even sound surprised. "We will come right home. We will leave tonight and be back tomorrow. How does that sound?"

Mike said it sounded great, a bit eagerly.

"Okay, we will see you soon, Mike."

Mike started to say bye and I love you, but then the line went imperiously dead.

He unclipped the earpiece and wedged it home, disconcerted. And confused: By the sound of Mom's voice, you'd think Mike had won the spelling bee, instead of her trip being bobtailed a couple days (and she had talked kind of funny, also, somehow too high and too perfect, like the President). But it didn't matter; they were coming home. He just hoped William would fix him dinner tonight, if the Sitter was still capable of such. He was hungry.

Like magic, Mike heard the insectile whir of William's cooling fan, coming by way of the living room, and the machine soon crept into the kitchen, still dressed in its farcical outfit.

"It's six o'clock, Michael. Suppertime," William said woodenly, and made for the pantry.

Mike agreed, requested some Hamburger Helper, and then removed himself to the living room. As the music of William's cooking poured from the kitchen, Mike started to calm, at last forgetting the last two days. It looked like everything was going to be okay, William's peculiarity notwithstanding.

Unknown to him, William had also just been on the phone.

***

The next morning, Mike again ignored his feckless alarm clock and William again ignored its duty; but it was Saturday, so it didn't matter. Mike awoke, well after nine, to find William once more in his room, jacked into the wall.

"Hey, Will," Mike said, slipping from the bed and out of his pjs, "how 'bout some breakfast?" He didn't expect results, given the thing's new meal-a-day quota, and he wasn't disappointed.

"Hello, Michael," was all William said. Its data port blinked curiously, receiving God knows what from the internet.

Another lightning bolt of anger pinged Mike's head, but it didn't amount to anything. Who needed William? Mom could cook breakfast like a champ, and she'd be home soon, if she wasn't already.

Mike, half-dressed and sleep-tousled, ducked into the hallway. "Mo-o-o-o-om!" he called into the house, but it went unrequited. He was a little ruffled by this—they should've been there by now—but he didn't let it bring him down. *Soon*, he thought. They'd be there soon. And, regardless, there were plenty more apples.

He had polished off one of them, then an orange, and then half of a second apple, before William galumphed downstairs. It came into the kitchen, its ludicrous dress unchanged, and Mike couldn't help but take a theatric bite in its presence, flaunting his independence. He *mmm*'ed. Good.

If William understood the gesture, it made no acknowledgement. It halted at the dinner table, obliquely dignified despite its confused clothing. Mike chewed.

"I have a secret, Michael," William said, foregoing greeting. The ruddy light pulsed five times, illuminating the brim of the homburg.

Mike nodded listlessly. Old news.

"I think you will like it, Michael," William said. "I think it will be—" An abrupt pause, then one more flash: "Fun."

Mike's eyes clouded; there was a falsity to William's speech. He likened it to a bully wheedling you around the corner so he can "show you something." Still, he chewed. The apple was good.

"Would you like to hear it, Michael?" the Sitter went on.

Mike shrugged bonelessly. "Yeah, I guess," he said, spuming apple on the *g*.

"Okay." The light blinked twice on that one—*Oh-kay*. "But first, you do must something for me." Pause. "Michael."

Mike's chewing slowed, and he swallowed uneasily: William was sounding *way* too much like a bully, now. He thought of the vagrant in the bathrobe, the wild, imploring eyes. "What?" Mike asked in a way that could be interpreted as rude but wasn't.

William raised its opaque right hand, shifting the turgid fabric of Dave's shirt. The hand held a folded slip of paper Mike hadn't noticed before; it went in front of him, over the table like a doily. William then instructed Mike on what to do, and Mike listened.

***

It was ten o'clock when Mike boarded the city bus, the day warming up. He felt small and awkward standing at the stop, alongside a man with long blond hair, and a big fat old woman who also had long blond hair, except hers was a wig. Then, when the bus hissed to a stop and its doors shot open, Mike became even smaller, like a mouse climbing the steps of that big building where Abe Lincoln lives. He was afraid the driver would stop him, even though William had coached him on what to say: he was going home, to Buford Avenue, he bussed all the time, and he was twelve, not nine. This fiction sounded about as real as a Marx mustache, and he knew no one would believe him, knew he'd get found out and taken back home (he'd felt very illicit these last couple days).

But no one stopped him. He just trotted onto the bus, dropped his coins in the weird bucket, and slunk into an open seat in the back, away from the blond man and the old woman and everyone else. He felt a little better when the bus started

121

moving, but was still far from comfortable. The worst was that he really didn't care about William's big stupid crazy secret, whatever it was, at least not enough to go to the mall like William had asked. Thing is, he thought William hadn't been asking at all, just like a bully trying to show you the imaginary thing around the corner so he can steal your lunch money: he had only agreed because he was *scared*, all told. But it didn't matter, none of it, because Mom and Dad would be back when he got home, and they'd know what to do about William, and Mike wouldn't have to put up with its bully-crap anymore.

One part of Mike's cover story was true, at least: he *was* heading for Buford Avenue, just to go to the radio store in the mall. When the sprawling sandstone mall crawled into view, he was afraid of getting collared on the way out, but, again, nobody said anything. Unbothered, he made his way into the mall and the radio store, its walls stocked with various doodads and gizmos. The place was empty but for a red-haired clerk sitting rigidly at the register, exuding self-importance.

Mike got the man's attention—a feat in itself—and handed him William's sheet of paper. "I need these," he said with shy curtness.

The unhappy-looking man accepted the slip of paper, consulted it, and then regarded Mike with that dubiety unique to redheads. "You want...these," he said flatly.

"Yep," Mike chirped, readying his story like a weapon.

The man's eyes danced between the extensive list of computer components, and the skinny brownette boy peeking over the counter.

"They're for my dad," Mike blurted, feeling *persona non grata*. "He sent me here to pick them up. For him. Because he's busy, and..." Mike trailed off, lost in the clerk's too-blue eyes.

There was a barbed pause. "You got money?" the man asked, finally.

Mike produced the three hundred-dollar bills William had given him—where William got them, he had no idea. He slapped them over the counter, gaining an odd satisfaction from calling the bluff.

The clerk, mellowing some at the sight of the money, stood from his stool. "Okay," he said, nodding. "Give me a minute."

He went to the back, carrying William's comprehensive list, and was gone longer than a minute.

**

Mike triumphantly quit the city bus, and started the few blocks home, swinging the swollen red radio-store bag. Despite being on what felt like a fool's errand—at the behest of a screwball Sitter, no less—there was a sense of accomplishment, a very adult feeling. Mom and Dad, who were surely home by now, would go bananas when he told them where he'd been, but he could pin it all on William. He would be sure to make a point of how scared and intimidated he'd felt, perhaps switching on the waterworks for good measure. All in all, he felt pleased with himself.

As for the goods themselves, they were all things Mike didn't recognize in the least, little computer chips and wires and a whole gaggle of -ometers. As big as the list had been, everything had fit in one bag. He did recognize one thing, though: an ear-clip phone, like the kind Mom and Dad had bought last year. This one was cheaper, a store-brand, but it was the same basic thing. Its package pressed against the semi-translucent bag, the woman on the box visible through a sensual red tint.

Two houses from his own, Mike saw a figure loitering by his fence, in the summer-lush arboretum that was his yard. He at first thought it was Dad— it was wearing Dad's clothes—but it was just William, standing inertly at the lawn's margin. The Sitter projected its usual aplomb, regarding Mike from afar. It reminded him of dogs he'd seen.

William made no initial reaction, but as Mike cleared the last house before his—the Vintners' Tudorish monstrosity—the machine stirred. Fixated on Mike, it matched his steps toward the gate, as though in imitation.

"Hi," Mike said awkwardly. The robot's movement was somehow predatory.

"Out there in the store, it accommodated you?" William asked.

Mike nodded despite the big word and weird syntax, passing sidelong glances at William. The two met at the gate, and before Mike could step through, the Sitter deftly relieved him of the red shopping bag. Then, without missing a step, William about-faced and bee-lined for the door; leaving Mike sweaty and empty-handed in the gate's jamb.

Mike watched it go, feeling something like robbed. The anger surfaced then, slow like a bubble in the mud. All that leg-work, and not so much as a thank you. Acting without thinking, he grabbed one of the pumice stones lining the flagstone walk, dandling it in his hand. He was tempted to let William have it, right in back of its gigantic head...but that seemed to be tempting fate, like teasing a man wearing a dynamite cummerbund, so he got William's attention the only other way he knew.

"Will, go fetch!" he called, then tossed the spongy stone to the lawn.

William didn't slow.

The anger heightened, becoming fire inside him. "*Hey!*" Mike barked, the word redoubling from the face of the house. "I said *go fetch*, you lousy piece of junk!"

William continued.

The anger vanished as quickly as it had arrived, waning into a crippling indifference. Mike slumped against the newel post. "But it's a *routine*, Will!" he whined, as though William had answered. His boney ribcage rose and fell. "You *have* to do it! I *order* you!"

With this, William stilled over the porch stairwell, his cocked pants leg revealing a slender gray calf. The machine's rotund head made a half-turn, discernable only by the homburg's movement. "I don't like that routine, Michael," it said, its mouth-light dulled in the daylight. The hat straightened, and the door banged.

Mike remained in the yard and, after several minutes, began to cry. However, he wasn't crying because William had refused to fetch, nor because his parent's blue minivan was still absent from the driveway. He cried because William's voice had carried a note of pure, burning hate.

**

Mike stayed outside. Some people passed, and he recognized one as Jamie Boyle's father. Mike waved but the man didn't notice. If asked, Mike would've said he was waiting for his parents, which was true. But no one asked. He got thirsty after an hour or so, but he could weather this. Fear trumped thirst. After two hours, however, he got hungry, and the two discomforts went in league, forming a keen irritation greater than the sum of its parts. So he went inside.

He prowled through the house, tiptoeing and peering around corners. William was nowhere to be found, and that suited him fine. In the kitchen, he opened the tap and drank, and the water was heavenly. He drank until his head hurt, then belched, and drank more. He'd worked up a thirst earlier, trekking back and forth from the mall, and it had since grown teeth. After confirming William's continued absence, he then migrated to the refrigerator, where he filched a pack of lunchmeat and a few wedges of cheese. Instead of eating in, he prudently carried these to the walk, to dine alfresco.

Chewing with bovine deliberation, he mused over what he should do, picking at the question of William with the cartoon dispassion of little boys. Considering it was going on three o'clock, one part of him concluded there was Something Wrong in regards to his parents, as they could have by now returned from Big Sur carrying the minivan on their backs. Another part of him was contrary, though, insisting that Mom and Dad would be there Soon, if he'd just wait. Besides, what could've happened to them?

Always one for the path of least resistance, Mike sided with the latter persuasion, and so remained over the walk, the overabundant vegetation his only company.

"Soon," he said out loud.

***

Hours passed, and Mike hadn't moved. As the light sighed and the shadows grew, he began to question his decision to wait things out.

Soon was a lie, he knew now. Mom and Dad weren't coming. Mom and Dad had lied. William had lied. William was a lie. Lies. He was confused, and his head hurt, too much sun. Then it came to him, and how simple it was: he would call Mom again. That would clear things up, right? And if Mom didn't pick up, he would call the police and report a harebrained Sitter. Simple. Win-win.

However, simple turned complicated as he stood on the stoop: the house appeared sinister, defiled, a monster-place. He grabbed for the door; pulled back; thought it over...then took the knob with two fingers, as though it would sting. His lower lip quivered a little as he opened the door.

The coast appeared clear, though the house had grown prematurely dark, thanks to the crush of vegetation crowding the lawn. After looking left and right, he whispered inside and eased the door shut. It at first moved silently, but then made an argumentative wooden snarl just before closing, seeming to disturb the entire house.

Mike froze, eyes squinched, awaiting some consequence to this; but there was nothing, and he at last latched the door. Then, after padding quietly through the living room, halfway to the kitchen, he heard footsteps from upstairs. Heavy footsteps.

He had a choice then: the kitchen and the phone, or back outside and a neighbor. He had time to kick himself for not considering a neighbor's in the first place, then the footsteps were thudding into the foyer, making the decision for him.

Abandoning subtlety, he scrambled for the kitchen and savaged the phone's earpiece from its base. He stabbed it over his ear; missed; fumbled it clumsily into place—then William eclipsed the doorway, making the kitchen darker. Mike "*ieee*'d" girlishly, his mind going blank.

The nefarious red light activated: "Hello, Michael." The fan buzzed, staving silence.

Mike managed a strained greeting and cowered by the fridge.

"What's wrong, Michael?" William asked, still looming in the jamb.

Mike blubbered something about lightning and going crazy.

"I'm not crazy, Michael," William said. "I feel." Pause. "Good."

William moved and Michael flinched. There was only one door into the kitchen.

William took another step and then equalized its legs, stopping feet away. "Don't be afraid, Michael. I just want to tell you my secret." Pause. That evil fan, eternal. "You helped me. So I'm keeping my promise. Remember?"

Mike nodded, lying. He knew nothing but his horrid present.

With a susurrus of small machinery and stretching fabric, William raised its right arm. In its uncuticled hand was a thin crescent of plastic with a bud at one end: an earpiece. A *phone*, like the one in the kitchen.

"Put this on, Michael," William said, assertive in spite of the monotone.

Mike accepted the gift, hesitantly, but when he went to put it on, something was wrong and it wouldn't fit—he still wore the other one, the phone he now wasn't going to use. In another universe, he may have laughed.

He slipped the old one off, and before he fit the new one on, he noticed it was different: William's had a little black cube taped on the side, with a length of red-and-green wire connecting it to the plastic bud that went into your ear. The cube was about

127

the size of a Matchbox car, large enough to house a few quarters. Or some of those computer chips from the radio store, maybe.

Though the box meant nothing to Mike, the sight of it repulsed him, and he was filled with an urge to drop the earpiece and hotfoot it out of there. He held the contraption uncertainly at his chest, looking between it and the door at William's back.

"It goes in your ear, Michael," William said, again with that slight air of demand. "Like the other one."

Feeling between a rock and a hard place, Mike took a deep breath and ratcheted the modified earpiece in place. He paused before driving it home, like Juliet holding the dagger... then he closed his eyes and popped the bud into his ear.

There followed a moment of psychosomatic upheaval, when Mike was sure the thing was melting his brain, striking it with the same miasmic lightning that had corrupted William. But then it passed, and he realized he was fine. There was some pressure on his ear, presumably from the added weight of the box, but that was all.

"Thank you," William said, and then raised its left hand. In it was a phone receiver, like the one on the counter, except William's was fixed with another of those little black boxes. A cable dangled from the receiver, also, spliced into the side.

"What's that for?" Mike asked, experimentally calm.

William answered by plugging the box into the slatted data port on its side, making it blink. There followed an enormous two seconds, Mike's eyes circuiting the antenna-box and William's not-face—then a shrill noise invaded his ear, brutally and impossibly loud. Like microphone feedback in a tin can. Like a million electric voices. Like all things ending.

His hands went to his ears, and there was time for a scream to start up his throat. Then he went stupendously still, and his hands dropped. He blinked heavily, and when the eyes opened, they were filled with nothing at all.

Mike looked himself up and down, then raised a tentative finger and dimpled his cheek, as though feeling it for the first time.

***

It was late Sunday afternoon when James Montgomery Boyle told his mom he was going for a ride around the neighborhood. She told him to be careful and watch for cars and wear his helmet and never talk to strangers, and, for God's sake, keep away from that delinquent Percy Skags's. And then he was gone, free.

It was a nice day, a little warm, but no scorcher. His bike, one of the new Schwinns, squeaked on the down cycle, the only sound in the lazy still. The artificial wind riffled his strawberry-blond hair, creating an illusion of great speed. He went jauntily down the way, passing the Howards's and the Conleys's and the Vintners's and the Bakers's, and then came to the roundabout terminating the street, what created a Moorish keyhole when seen from above. He'd started through, for the other side of the street, when he remembered his mom's admonition to steer clear of the Skags' place.

Slowing, he made a sloppy U-turn and backtracked the way he'd come. Then, after again passing the big steeply Howard house—his mom called it a "Victorian," though there was nothing victorious about it—he stopped, at the Conley place. James had been wrestling with how he'd called Mike a liar that Friday. It made him feel kind of sick, and he thought he ought to apologize. It was wrong of him, he knew, and besides, if he cut himself off from Mikey, who would he swap Wii games with?

He parked his squeaky Schwinn at the gate, then covered the little jungle that had eaten the Conleys' lawn over the last couple years. It was all trees and flowers, and vines creeping up trellises and monkey-bar pergolas; he fancied you could get lost in there. The green was so thick, once he got to the house, he felt miles away from home. It was kind of neat, but kind of spooky, too.

He knocked twice; waited; knocked again. When this yielded no response, he noticed the windows were dark, and the empty driveway. It looked as though his apology would have to wait.

Then there was a noise from his right, and he turned to find none other than Michael Conley, standing in the shadowy alameda that circled the house.

"Mikey! Just who I was looking for..." James started, but tapered off when he saw that Michael had company: there were others with him, kids, about ten by James' count. They clumped subordinately behind Michael like a band of lemmings. James recognized a few from around the neighborhood, but the majority were foreign. A couple even looked to be older, teenagers—Big Kids. James was enthralled.

"Hey, you havin' a party or somethin'?" he asked, and the question left a sour taste in his mouth—if so, why wasn't *he* invited? Had Mikey taken their fight worse than he thought?

"Come here, James," Michael said, and James went board-stiff: Mikey sounded different. His voice was thicker, deeper, seeming to belong to the high-schoolers at his wing. And his words carried, too, like an announcer on TV.

"You okay, Mikey?" James said, obediently starting toward the crowd. "You sound kinda..." There was no word for it.

Michael said nothing.

As James neared Michael and his little flock, which had neither spoken nor moved, James noted things depending from their ears. He couldn't really make them out, due to the heavy shade, but they looked like big weird earrings of some sort, maybe something a pirate would wear.

James hopped the porch and joined them in the verdant little forest, the canopy lending insularity too complete to be comfortable. Feeling suddenly awkward, he said: "I just came by, to, uh, apologize—"

"Put this on, James," Michael said, again with that alien voice. He extended one of the funny-looking earrings they all wore, shoving it nearly under James's nose. Michael moved kind of weird, James thought, all stiff and fitful, kind of like a Sitter—a *lot* like a Sitter, actually.

James regarded the earring with askance, almost crossing his eyes to do so. His hand rose in degrees and he limply accepted it, callipering it in two fingers. "Whaz'it do?"

"It's a secret, James," Michael said. He was staring in a way James didn't like.

James looked dumbly to the earring, then to the crowd of kids, appealing for help and receiving none. Their eyes burned cold over him, vaguely carnivorous; also, they seemed to have closed around him without him realizing it. It crossed his mind to politely return Mikey's strange gift and make for his Schwinn, but now that peer pressure had reared its head, denial was strictly out of court.

With a spry shrug, James raised the earring and slipped it over his ear. It was a little heavy, but it fit.

ZERO

Escarg-O

By Chantal Boudreau

Steve had to battle his way back into the kitchen through the swarming throng of women that had gathered at the back of the Crystal Fountain Bistro. The establishment was a trendy and expensive gourmet restaurant that had always been reasonably popular, but now, because the gothic alternative rock singer-celebrity, Mars Grimm, had chosen to make it his preferred hang-out, it was "the" place to be. Those of his groupies and more zealous fans who could not actually get into the bistro made a point of hovering around both the front and back doors, hoping to at least get a glimpse of their musical idol. That was why Steve had been forced to shove his way through the mob after hoisting garbage into the dumpster in the back alleyway. Crowd control was not part of the job description of a prep cook.

"This is crazy," he muttered, as he passed Ray, the second cook on shift that night. Ray was older than Steve, who was a fresh-faced blond-haired young man just out of culinary school. Ray, on the other hand, was a tall, dusky, lanky man whose skin was creased with wrinkles because of his heavy smoking and too much exposure to the sun in his youth. "I mean, I know the business he brings in is gold, but you can't move out there, and I actually had to beat some of them back from the door to get it closed."

"You think you've got it bad," Ray grumbled, as he tossed shallots in hot oil in a skillet. "Doug told me that I'm being promoted to procurement. He says that Phillip is too busy planning out the menu, organizing the kitchen, prepping the staff roster and cooking the main entrees and special deserts. Our master chef doesn't have the time to hunt out suppliers who can offer us quality foods, and the manager doesn't think he has the qualifications to fill in for that role himself—he's all about the finances and dealing with the latest problems caused by our increased popularity, like the need for more security."

"We have suppliers already—what the hell are you talking about?" Steve asked, as he washed and disinfected his hands in the utility sink. His shoulders were still tense from the stressful experience outside.

"We have fabulous suppliers, and that's one of the reasons why the food here has the reputation it does for being such high quality, but what those suppliers offer is limited, to some extent. I'm supposed to find things that are novel, extreme and out of the ordinary, the kind of things that might be considered delicacies that no other restaurant in town serves. That's a hard demand to meet because of the sheer number of food establishments around the city. Some of them are pretty oddball too. You'll find restaurants in the surrounding area that offer almost anything. I've been digging, but I haven't come up with anything yet, and I'm starting to feel desperate," Ray replied, returning the pan to the stove. The shallots sizzled. "It's all because of this Mars Grimm guy, too. This could cost me my job."

Steve didn't like the sound of that. Ray was the only other member of the staff he actually liked; he was laid-back and down-to-earth. Everyone else, the whole stuck-up lot of them, he just tolerated.

"What's wrong with what we have? There's a reason why Mars started coming here and we don't have anything bizarre on the menu. Why would we want to change it?" he protested.

"Like I said...Mars Grimm. Management wants to keep him as a regular patron. I heard he has a pattern, and that he doesn't like to eat the same thing twice, just like he doesn't like to sleep with the same woman more than once. Once he gets tired of what we have to offer, he'll move on to somewhere new, and all of the publicity that he brought us will go with him. Let that happen and we'll be yesterday's news. If we want him to keep coming back, we have to have something new for him every time he visits—the more unusual the better. We're serving him quail eggs in the chef's special sauce today, presented in sauteed nests made from grated sweet potatoes and gruyere, with his usual side order of escargot, flash-fried in extra virgin olive oil with garlic and shallots."

For some strange reason, Mr. Grimm had a penchant for snails. It was the only food that he would eat repetitively, and it was the thing that had drawn him to the bistro in the first place. "Phillip has a few more things he can experiment with, but he has already tapped out all his of connections in Louisiana. We need to think more exotic, but when it comes to that I'm clueless. I'm a boy from the farm belt. I like good food, and I can cook better than Phillip can when it comes to domestic fare, but exotic cuisine?"

Ray shook his head and tossed his spatula on the counter in a disheartened gesture.

"I might be able to help you, if you don't mind going black market," Steve offered, reaching for a large knife and some cloves of garlic.

"I'll try anything at this point. It took me a long time to get used to this kitchen and Phillip's way of doing things. He was the only one willing to give me a break, because I don't have the proper culinary background. If he fires me, I'm done for. I'll never get another restaurant job around here, not unless you call slinging hash in a diner a restaurant job. What did you have in mind?"

"I have a friend that lives in my building who imports exotic plants and animals. He does it illegally, usually for decoration or pets, not for food, but I can put in a special request for things that will be edible."

This "friend" also imported drugs, but Steve decided not to mention that. Steve had provided the fellow with early warning that the cops were dropping in on two occasions, and as a result, this friend owed him.

"As long as we are willing to pay top dollar, he can supply the goods. If it's weird and wonderful and not something that you can get around here, my friend can procure it for us," Steve assured Ray. "It'll just be a matter of doing a little research to figure out the best way to cook whatever he gives us, or we can foist that responsibility on Phillip, since he dumped this one on you."

Steve was wondering if their head chef had done that to Ray on purpose, expecting the second cook to fail so that he had a scapegoat to blame when Mars Grimm eventually left them. He had hired Ray begrudgingly, and although the man was an extremely hard worker with a miraculously refined eye and taste for the gourmet, Phillip was still put off by his rustic sensibilities.

"Do you think that will work? What if we accidentally end up with something poisonous?" The thin man swallowed hard. He didn't trust anything that wasn't home grown.

"You leave all of that to me. Nothing poisonous, I'll make sure of that—just things bizarre enough to knock Mars Grimm's socks off."

Steve set about chopping up the garlic. It had to be fresh – anything else was unforgivable. He watched a flustered and still gloomy-looking Ray continue to fidget his way nervously around the kitchen. He still doubted that Steve could yield the kind of results he needed to keep his head off of the chopping block, but he didn't exactly have any other option. He would put his fate in the prep cook's hands and hope for the best.

***

Wherever Mars Grimm went, he was pursued by flocks of fans who had to be fended off by the efforts of his entourage. He liked to eat alone however, and he had ever since his high school days, before he had ever come up with his current persona. The last time he had eaten in a restaurant with anyone was in eleventh grade when he had gone to the only French restaurant in his home town, the Plume d'Oree, with his high school crush, Cindy Landowski. It had been their first date, as well as their only date. But that was back when he was known as Marvin Grimley, and what seemed like an eternity ago.

Mars Grimm was only a stage name, but he had carried it for so long that it was now as much a part of who he was as

Marvin Grimley. As he sat at his table at the bistro, an exclusive spot in a sheltered niche of the restaurant, he thought of that date with Cindy, sipping his drink and waiting for his appetizer to arrive. He remembered it well, one of the most rewarding nights for him ever, as well as one of the most devastating. She had been the pastor's daughter and he was a scrawny little goth punk, hardly an appropriate match.

Cindy had not been the typical teen-aged girl, neither over made-up nor under-dressed. She was very proper, always dressing in loosely-fitting sweaters or high-collared shirts that didn't expose any cleavage, dress pants or long skirts with hems that extended down below her knees, and flat-heeled close-toed, sensible shoes. All of her clothing had been neutral-colored or plaid – she had never worn anything bright or flashy. She had also kept her plain brown hair tied back; looking-very prim and giving him a good view of her pale-skinned face. She was not model-pretty; her cheeks were a little too round and plump, her nose was somewhat angular and freckles dotted the bridge and the spaces just beneath her eyes. What had actually captivated Marvin was her eyes, very wide, very green and haunted to some degree. It was because of those eyes that he had been smitten.

Cindy hadn't exactly ignored him at first; Cindy didn't ignore anyone. She was polite, and she had been quite receptive, to greeting him in the hall, but there was always a coolness about her; not just directed towards Marvin, but towards everyone, like she was trying to keep the world at a distance. Marvin was like that too, but he actively avoided everyone but his goth friends and Cindy. It hadn't been exactly difficult. One look at his piercings, his black lipstick, his heavy mascara and his blue streaked-spiked hair and most of the students at his high school had given him a wide berth—almost everyone but Cindy.

It had been three months after the start of tenth grade that he had managed to work up the nerve to say anything to her beyond hello. He had figured she had only ever spoken to him before then to be courteous to him, because it was part of being a good Christian.

Then one lunch hour he had found himself loitering in front of the school library with her, waiting to be let in. He had never been so nervous in his life, but she was holding a book in her hands that he had read and loved, a dystopian novel that vilified science and genetic experimentation. They had had different reasons for reading it. He had read it for the futuristic gloom and doom and she had read it because she was a creationist who was convinced that genetic experimentation was a sin, an attempt from man at playing God. Nevertheless, it had given them something in common, and a reason to strike up a conversation. They had only spoken for a few moments, until the library doors had been unlocked, but it had been a start and had loosened Marvin's tongue for future encounters.

Marvin had recognized that they would make an unusual pairing. She was demure and respectful, although not timid in any way, and he was sarcastic and edgy, but that had not deterred him. He had made a point of actually speaking to her more at length every time he had run into her after that and eventually, he had grown comfortable enough around her to invite her on casual friendly outings with him. She had always politely declined, but Marvin had been convinced that it was only a matter of time, along with the right event and his continued persistence, before she would agree to a platonic date. *If he could win that victory*, he had thought, *then he had hope of taking her on a real date someday.*

Finally, one day in the eleventh grade, although Cindy had said no again for the umpteenth time, things had taken a much different course after her refusal. Marvin had turned to walk away, discouraged but still not defeated, when she had reached out after him and grasped his arm. He had frozen and glanced back at her. She had never touched him before.

"I can't go out with a boy on a date unless they ask my father for permission first. I wish he already knew you like I do, but he doesn't and I don't think he'd approve of the way you look. I'm sorry, Marvin. He's only trying to protect me. He wants what's best for me. He wants me to marry a kind and sensible God-fearing man someday."

Mars was disturbed from his reminiscing as his appetizer arrived. He picked at it, but he barely put a dent in it. They had brought him an Asian salad with a variety of unidentifiable greens as well as white radish, mandarin slices and a ginger sesame dressing—a tasty enough combo. It was well-prepared, but he was so lost in his thoughts that he did not really appreciate it.

He—well, the him who was Marvin—had talked Cindy into setting up a meeting with her father. He had cleaned up well, slicking back his hair so the blue was hardly noticeable, removing any studs from his piercings and making sure he wore something that covered his multiple tattoos. The suit he had worn had actually made him look very respectable; it was one he had been forced to acquire for a family wedding. When he had set out to meet with Cindy's father, Marvin had been determined to win him over.

The pastor had been very old school, a stern looking man with a heavy Eastern European accent. His excessively cool demeanor had made Cindy seem particularly warm and fuzzy in comparison. Marvin had known that he would have to prove himself and his good intentions, so he was not surprised when the man had begun to grill him with question after question. Marvin had answered very cautiously, choosing his words carefully. As much as the pastor had tried to find fault with him, Marvin had been even more resolved not to falter under pressure, and when the interrogation was done, Marvin was victorious. Father Landowski had agreed to let Cindy go out on a date with him, but there were conditions.

"To prove that you are not acting on the impulse of infatuation, you will have to take Cindy somewhere very special. Dating should be reserved to mature young adults, which means you should be bringing her to an appropriately mature venue. You do not escort my daughter to fast food and a crass picture show. You accompany her to a gourmet meal and something sophisticated like the ballet, or the theatre. I hope that I do not have to remind you that a real man picks up the tab without expecting anything in return. And there is to be no touching. You may take her hand, but nothing else."

Marvin had agreed to his conditions, and that was why the pair had ended up at the Plume d'Oree. It was the best meal of his life; he had eaten their specialty, escargot, and now he relived the feelings of that evening every time he ate them again. He could not look at a snail without thinking of Cindy. He had tried to find another food that would offer him some other equally strong sensation, something that would offer just as powerful a pleasure, and distract him from her memory, but so far he had failed at this quest.

Mars pushed the salad plate, still more than half full, aside. His server would clear it away in seconds and his entree would be moments behind that. There would be snails accompanying the main dish. He craved those snails like a drug. He needed them.

After dinner on that fateful day long ago, he had not taken Cindy to the ballet or the theatre. Instead, he brought her to an outdoor orchestral concert playing in the gazebo at the park, and then for a moonlight stroll alongside of the lake there. She had seemed more open and warmer than she had been in the past, taken by the fact that Marvin had actually convinced her father to allow their date, and charmed by the romantic atmosphere of the restaurant. She had gripped Marvin's hand invitingly as they had walked in the deepening shadows. Her skin had been flushed and he had been able to feel her racing pulse through contact with her wrist. When they paused beside the water, she had captured him with those bewitching emerald eyes in the moonlight. He had not been able to help himself and soon realized that he was going to break one of her father's rules. He had leaned forward to kiss her.

What exactly had he been expecting? That she would not see it coming and be stunned by his advances? That she would see it coming, and take offense, retreating quickly? That she might even slap him to warn him away? All of those things he could have anticipated. Instead, Cindy had not only met him half way, but she had pulled him in closer, hungrily. Marvin had been the one who had been stunned, especially when she, after kissing him several times, had started unbuttoning his shirt. If he had been in his right mind, he would have batted her hands away before she had opened up his shirt to expose the pale skin of his chest to the moonlight. There was a tattoo there, right over his heart, that he had not wanted her to see. It was a demonic symbol, a pentagram with an upside-down cross and a grinning devil face, an image that was popular in goth circles— an image now popular with fans of Mars Grimm. But not with Cindy.

She had let out a stifled scream, recoiling away from that small patch of ink, her expression filled with shock. Stumbling back, she had dropped her arms to her side and had shaken her head vigorously.

"No—no, what am I doing? That mark...you are a tool of the Devil, sent here to tempt me into sin, and I was about to fall for it. How could I let myself fall for that? My father was right...I'm better off alone, until he finds me the right man."

She had turned and run off before Marvin had been able to stop her.

Mars retreated once more from his memories. Through his silk shirt, he touched that spot on his chest where the tattoo could still be found. She had taken to avoiding him after that, all because of a silly picture that he wore that happened to be popular with his friends. Marvin had been no Satanist, nor was Mars one now—an athiest then, yes, and a hedonist now, very much so, but he couldn't have been a Devil-worshipper because he didn't believe in the Devil.

Marvin had been heartbroken. It had been very sad— after that one date, Marvin had been completely in love and Cindy was no longer even his friend. She still said hello if they bumped into each other in the hall, but her enchanting green eyes no longer met his gaze and she was quiet, speaking the word with a wary edge and saying nothing more. He thought he would get over it eventually, when he finished high school, went off to college and then began to pursue his musical dreams, but there would be no peace or end of longing for him. That was why he ate escargot with every meal, because it reminded Mars of that date with Cindy. It was also why he insisted on a new dish at every meal. He wanted to find some sort of food of the gods that would bring him the type of euphoria to fill that soul-piercing hole, and rid him of that persistent emptiness. None of it ever did, and he often left his meals unfinished because they failed to bring him the gut-numbing salvation he sought.

That yearning for Cindy was also why Mars bedded a new woman every night. Because of his celebrity, he was never at a loss for a partner. He kept hoping that he would finally come across a woman who would make him want to forget Cindy, but he never did. He had been with ladies of all types, shapes and backgrounds, from the fresh-faced girls who flocked to his dark and morbid concerts to rebel against their parents, to the die-hard goth chicks with more tattoos and piercings than he could count as they lay in a tangled heap in his sheets. It was a temporary distraction, a small burst of pleasure for a man still plagued since adolescence by a broken heart. He blamed himself for falling for a girl who was living in a different world, untouchable for someone like him. Mars could have almost anything he wanted, but he had never truly had her, and that was all he seemed to ever really want.

He could have tried losing himself in drugs and alcohol. It was almost expected of him, but that would only dull the ache within, not kill it. That, and it might actually make him lose some of what he remembered of Cindy, and he didn't want that —not unless he could replace her altogether. Self-medicating wasn't the answer, anymore than any of the other self-destructive behaviors he practiced, so he had stood firm against the stereotype and remained clean and sober.

Mars pushed the shaggy dark hair that hung over his heavily black-traced eyes out of his face, as they set the day's dish in front of him. It was creative, cutesy little nests and sauced eggs, all edible, but two spoonfuls of the decadent meal and he knew that it would not bring him the fulfillment he desired. Neither could his fame, his wealth, his publicists or all of the personal stylists and trainers in the world. For a life that appeared to be so full, it was actually quite vacant. He pushed people away on purpose. Most believed it to be part of the Mars

Grimm persona, but that wasn't it at all. He pushed them all away because they could never really understand him.

There was one thing there on his plate that he eagerly devoured, despite his disinterest in the entree. Mars let each bite linger for a moment in his mouth so that he could savor its rich, garlicky goodness. Then he would chew each little succulent morsel until they had disintegrated in his mouth. As he ate, memories of the dinner shared with Cindy at the Plume d'Oree flooded his mind and he basked in that thrill, that desire, that hope that had been lost to him for so long. He was always mournful when he got to the last forkful. He knew most of the staff at the bistro thought him strange, or perhaps "eccentric" since he was rich and famous, but he hadn't cared what other people thought of him since the point where he had left his hometown, and any dreams of recovering Cindy, behind.

"The meal, Mr. Grimm, it was not to your liking?" his server asked, arriving to find the dish mostly untouched. "The chef could prepare you something else, in its place." He looked anxious and unnerved, the way most people did when they encountered Mars face-to-face. Mars stared the tense-looking man in the eye.

"No—I've lost my appetite. Same old, same old," he responded bitterly.

He knew that the man would find his reply disturbing, and word would get back to the kitchen. Mars would make sure that he left his server a hcfty tip, nevertheless. It certainly wasn't the suave little man's fault that Mars had once again failed to find satisfaction. Tossing the money on the table, he slid his chair back, stood, and headed out in search of that evening's entertainment.

***

"I hope you have something good for me tonight, Steve," Ray said with more than a hint of exasperation in his voice. "He turned his nose up at everything we served him for the last two weeks before he went out of town; from the spider monkey

143

brains to the roasted capybara. How much more exotic does he want us to get?"

"Ah—but he keeps coming back, and that's what counts. Anyway, I think I have a real winner tonight. You know how much he loves snails. I don't think he'll be disappointed with the special dish we'll present to him this fine evening," Steve stated, somewhat smugly. He lifted an unusual clay container out of the hemp bag he had brought in with him, and placed it down carefully on the stainless steel countertop.

"Snails? More snails? But he always orders the escargot as a side-dish anyway. Why would he want even more snails?" Ray wrinkled his Romanesque nose in disgust. Of all the gourmet foods he had ever prepared, he had understood least the appeal of escargot. Even prepared with great finesse they were still rubbery flavorless balls of flesh that happen to absorb the taste and aroma of anything that they were cooked in: garlic, butter, wine…whatever. He considered them an unpleasant dining experience based on texture alone.

Steve chuckled gleefully, with a wicked gleam in his eyes. "Oh, but Ray, these aren't just any snails. Get a load of this."

He tilted he pot and gently shook its contents out onto the tabletop. A handful of snails, still alive, oozed on its shiny surface. Ray could immediately see that they were no ordinary escargot. Their eyestalks rippled and pulsated with a spotty and almost fluorescent green glow—a disturbingly vibrant display. Ray staggered back towards the utility sink, with his hand over his mouth and turning almost the same shade of green as the snails' eyestalks.

"Aw geez, Steve! That's disgusting! Where the hell did those things come from....Africa? The Amazon? Why would anyone in their right mind want to eat those things?"

Steve was laughing with great enthusiasm by this point.

"Believe it or not, I brought you domestic goods this time, ole boy, from right here in the U. S. of A. Those are home grown, from parts of the farm belt—*Novisuccinea ovalis*. I think that's how you pronounce it. And as far as being in his right mind, I don't think our Mars Grimm qualifies there. He has got to be one of the bigger obsessive compulsive celebrities out there."

Ray was shocked. He leaned in a little closer to get a better look at them, but not too close.

"Those things are from my home turf? I've never seen anything like it. How are we supposed to cook them?"

The younger man hesitated, looking a little less self-assured.

"Well, I was thinking we'd serve them raw."

"Raw?!" The word came out as more of a squawk. "Are you crazy?!!"

"Well, they serve sushi raw, don't they? And we have to keep them alive to maintain the special effects. That's the whole point, isn't it—a weird novelty food? Mars will love them. He hasn't turned away a snail that we've put in front of him yet."

Steve chose not to tell Ray that he and his supplier had experimented with various dosages of drugs to find the right amount to stun the snails without killing them, so that they wouldn't be all squirmy on the plate. The only movement Mars would see would be the pulsating of the eyestalks, which came from the larvae, the brown-banded broodsac, burrowed inside them and not the snail proper.

"Raw snails? Are you sure that's hygienic? If a major celebrity comes down with food poisoning from our restaurant, the health inspectors will shut us down without blinking an eye, and our reputation will be shot. I don't know..." Ray said, drawing in a sharp breath.

"It'll be fine. They get eaten alive by birds all the time—plain old robins. They just poop the things out and go about their business. They don't get sick. Besides, my supplier tested them out himself. He ate them raw, and he never felt better." Raw, but dead, the eyestalk pulsations having ceased as well, because the broodsacs within had also perished. Those had been the snails that had failed their little drug test and succumbed to overdose. Steve's friend had volunteered to eat them, not wanting to waste good drugs. The experiment had left the man high as a kite but otherwise healthy.

Ray gazed at the creatures unhappily. He had a nauseating feeling that this was a very bad idea, but if they didn't come up with a win soon, he was toast. He decided he had to risk it.

"Let me talk to Phillip about it and get him on board," Steve continued. "I'll even prepare them. You and he won't have to go near them. I'll handle everything." Steve had already gotten over his initial revulsion at the sight of the obscene-looking gastropods, and now just thought that they were fascinating.

Ray conceded, eager to wash his hands of the entire creepy affair. It was far beyond his personal comfort zone.

Steve chuckled internally. He was certain this would earn him some recognition, and maybe fast-track him to a position as sous-chef. He would be preparing a meal fit for a king – well, at least a goth-rock king.

*****

Mars was in a much fouler mood than usual, just getting back from a two month tour that had been exhausting and personally unrewarding. His music producer had demanded it, as a means of promoting his latest CD release, but being on the road often limited his food choices as well as his bedmates and wore on his nerves. He hadn't slept or eaten well, and was looking haggard for it, the dark circles under his eyes offsetting his pale skin. He had also lost about ten pounds, something his slender frame could barely afford. He ached for his escargot and a place that felt familiar.

He tried not to be sour with the maitre d' but his hunger overrode courtesy and he snapped at the man when there was a minor delay with getting him in and seated. He wolfed the crawfish bisque they brought him with greater fervor than he normally displayed towards food and was on his third espresso by the time his entree arrived, downing the thick brown liquid like it was ambrosia.

The server entered his niche carrying a covered serving platter, not the usual presentation for Mars' meals. He placed it on the table before Mars, who trembled with anticipation, not to mention the jitteriness from his espressos. He leaned forward as the server removed the cover, and then lurched back, startled, equally as quick when he saw what was there.

"What the hell!"

"You said you wanted things that were very different, Mister Grimm, and our chef knows how much you enjoy your escargot. He has prepared for you an extra-special dish of escargot, one, no doubt, like no other you've ever seen before. Is it too much? Shall I return it to the kitchen? I'm sure the chef will prepare something else for you, a little more ordinary—a little less extreme."

Mars sat back in his chair, blinking rapidly. He had never seen any meal like it and it made his heart catch in his throat. The bottom of the platter was liberally layered with garlic butter, and bright green steamed asparagus, drizzled in hollandaise sauce, had been carefully placed in a pattern that covered the entire dish. Positioned purposefully in the various spaces bare of spears were the snails; their vibrantly-colored pulsating eyestalks could not fail to catch Mars's own eyes. They were mesmerizing, the same brilliant shade as the eyes of his lost love, but they surged and swelled with unnatural light and patterns. It was sort of like looking at drug-related animation from the sixties. He drew in a deep breath.

"No," he said, his voice choked with emotion and his mouth filled with saliva. His stomach rumbled to remind him just how hungry he was. "These are perfect—perfect."

The server left Mars to enjoy his meal in solitude. At first he just sat, glued to his seat and staring. A part of him was completely repulsed at the notion of eating these things that looked like alien gastropods from another planet, but a second part was fascinated by the frightening meal and ravenous, and a third part, the self-destructive part liked the idea of taking his chances, pumping extra adrenaline into his espresso-wired veins.

Finally, Mars managed to muster the nerve to reach for one of the snails. He jabbed his two-pronged tiny fork into it, and was surprised at how difficult it was to separate the snail meat from the shell; normally they yielded quite easily. Tensing up, he closed his eyes and brought it to his mouth. He bit down.

Mars was startled at the unusual taste, mostly disguised by the aromatic salty flavor of the garlic butter, and the texture, very different from his usual escargot side dish. After two chews—that were unpleasant in some indefinable way—he swallowed the rest of that first snail mostly whole. His eyes opened wide as he thought he felt something wriggle at the back of his throat, and the idea made him gag and reach for his drink, barely able to keep it down.

He waited for a moment, not finding the experience at all similar to that evening at the Plume d'Oree, but not deterred immediately by this. Mars wanted to see if he would have a good response in the end, as the snail settled in his stomach, and if he would find something that would fill that gaping painful hole within him. He wasn't expecting much, and when at first he felt nothing different, he leaned forward to push the dish away in disgust, but before his fingertips could make contact with the platter something did change.

It started at first with a slight numbness in his stomach, one that dulled the edge of his hunger pangs and washed away the sense of malaise that he typically felt. Next came the euphoria, one that originated from the pit of his belly and gradually striated out to his head and his extremities, bringing with it lusty thoughts and bizarre fantasies that instantly sprung to mind. Finally, there was the head trip, like Mars had dropped acid and was having the best high of his life—one giant mind fuck. And at the centre of it all was a constant stream of memories of Cindy and her delicious kisses.

Mars felt better than he had in years, and stretched back in his chair with a blissful moan, watching swirls of color dance around the room and sensing his pants tighten around his groin. There was no discomfort, only pure delight. He rested like this for several minutes drawing in deep breaths and staring, relaxed, up at the ceiling while wearing a smile of deep satisfaction. Then, he eventually remembered that there were more snails on the platter. Sitting up abruptly, and ignoring the asparagus completely, he started rapidly shoveling the remainder of the snails into his mouth, as quickly as he could manage. He did not take the time to even chew, swallowing each of them whole. He did not shy at the tickle in his throat this time, enjoying the sensation instead of balking at it. This was the food he had been looking for. This was his paradise.

Mars did not stick around for desert, or for his after-dinner coffee, which he rarely left without. He did not touch the meal other than the snails either. Dropping enough money to cover three times what they had brought him that evening, he surged out of his chair and began to stagger his way towards the main exit. He was finding it difficult to walk straight, a fog settling over his mind even as the colors and patterns continued to swirl and dip throughout his line of vision. He found himself losing all thoughts, his sense of self disintegrating as he headed for his limo, leaving behind only the strongest compulsion to accompany his mindless euphoria—he had to be with Cindy again.

He was oblivious to the girls who succeeded in getting past security and pursued him to the car, responding to the fact that he seemed blissfully stoned and aware of his clear arousal at that moment. They were disappointed as he slammed the door in their faces, almost crushing one woman's hand in the process. He then had his driver speed away. It was the first time that Mars Grimm had left the bistro unaccompanied by whomever he had chosen from the gathered group of fans to be his willing plaything for the night.

Those who were not as close as the girls who had forced their way past the guards did not feel as disappointed. Watching Mars from more of a distance, they had all noticed that he was not his normal self, and not just because he was drunk or stoned. He had moved with sluggish jerky steps, his arms hanging limply at his side like he was unsure how to use them. It reminded the majority of them of some undead creature rising from the grave. He had not eyed the mob even once, focused entirely on his destination. Those who did manage to get a good look at his face turned away in discomfort, chills running down their spine. The goth star's visage was unnaturally placid, bearing an expression that seemed almost inhuman, and not only did his eyes appear soulless, there was a faint green glow to them, pulsating rhythmically. Some thought it was all special effects, a sad grab for even more media attention, like he didn't have enough. But the true goth girls, the ones who recognized a summoning from Death himself, knew that there was only one word to describe what their musical idol had become...

Zombie.

***

Cindy Zimmer, nee Landowski, sat all alone at her kitchen table nursing a once scalding but now lukewarm cup of tea. Her husband, Caleb, was out at an all-male Bible study meeting, and her children had gone off to visit their paternal grandparents, who lived in a neighboring town, for the weekend. It would be another lonely night in a house devoid of any real means of entertainment. She could listen to some of her Christian music CDs, start up some new craft project for the next church bazaar, or prepare for her own Bible study group that met later in the week, but the truth was, all of those things bored her to tears.

She'd had a chance once to escape the dreary life that she led, to branch off to a much more interesting and unpredictable path, and she had grabbed anxiously at the first excuse to flee from it. For someone who had been preached to about faith all of her life, she had never been one to demonstrate much of it, especially when it had come to trusting her own instincts.

She reached over to the daily newspaper that rested on the opposite end of the table and flipped it over. Just as she was expecting, *his* face was there again—but his face was always there, scattered everywhere as if to purposefully rub salt in old wounds. It wasn't as if she hadn't wanted him back then; in fact, she had loved almost everything about him. She had liked his air of rebellion and brooding moods, even though he was truly a sweet and gentle creative soul, and she had adored their talks in the hallway, stirring and heartfelt. Although nobody had ever been mean to her, he had been the only one who had ever demonstrated an active interest in her. No one else in her life really had, other than to make sure that she was following their rules. Marvin, however, had never demanded anything from her. He had offered her affection while respecting her feelings and not expecting anything in return.

Life, fate, hadn't been fair in molding them to be so different, and in causing her father to be so closed minded. *She* hadn't been fair in that she had let her own fears and insecurities drive a wedge between them, and not because she had been worried about her father's reaction. It had been her own level of passion and the intensity of her feelings, emotional and physical, that had frightened her and had caused her to withdraw from him. Marvin had moved on, found his place in the world, become Mars Grimm—the star, lived his dream and now had his pick of women to make love to. He got to travel to exciting places and live in a big city far from his original home.

Cindy, on the other hand, scared little rabbit that she was, had abandoned all idea of doing what she really wanted. She had remained in her home-town, married the man her father had chosen for her, and started having kids when her husband had declared that the time was right. She loved her children, but once they were grown and gone she would have nothing. She didn't think that it was possible, but Caleb was colder and more reserved than her father was and not a man she would have ever chosen for herself.

Whenever she saw Marvin's picture, she would start daydreaming about who she could have been, all of the experiences she could have shared with a man who actually loved her. Even if he had truly been a tool of the Devil, tempting her to stray from the flock, how much worse would it have been than being alive on the outside, but dead on the inside?

She was so lost in thought that she practically jumped out of her skin when the phone rang. Caleb was slightly deaf and kept the ringer on high, so Cindy always found the shrill sound somewhat startling. She actually hesitated a moment before picking it up, assuming it must be a telemarketer or her mother, the only people who ever called her. At first, all she heard on the other end was breathing, and she was about to hang up, thinking that it was an obscene caller, but then there was a voice —a familiar one.

"Come to me."

Cindy sat up and tightened her grip on the phone. She doubted that it was actually him, maybe just her mind playing tricks on her because of her wishful thinking. She swallowed hard.

"W-what?" she stammered. "Who is this?"

"Meet me."

His voice was a little slurred, like he'd been drinking. The media had never suggested that Mars was a drug-user or a lush, and Cindy was quite certain that they would have if that were the case. The paparazzi would have loved that kind of ammunition for a smear campaign; that was why his irreverent womanizing was so well-known.

"Is this Marvin?"

"I need to see you."

There was no expression to his words and his tone was a little hushed and garbled. To call out of the blue – she wondered if he was severely depressed. She had heard that that often happened to artists and musicians, and being into all of that gothic stuff and singing dreary songs about death? She shuddered. Maybe Marvin was contemplating suicide and would do something horrible if she didn't go see him.

"I can't go to LA, Marvin. I'm married now. I have kids."

"I'll come to you."

A few words, brief but gravelly, and then silence. Cindy wasn't sure if she should do this. She desperately wanted to see Marvin again and apologize for the way she had treated him after their date. She also wanted to look at his pretty face, because he was pretty as opposed to handsome, and feel that old thrill run through her again. If he was considering suicide, she wanted to talk him down, in a non-preachy way, and convince him to get professional help. She would have to come up with an excuse for her husband. If Marvin were coming right away, he could probably arrive by the following afternoon, so the kids would still be at their grandparents...

"Well, if you're willing to come here, I can see you. There's a coffee shop not far from my house, a Cowboy Joe's. We could meet there. There's no harm in two old friends getting together to talk about old times, and to be honest with you, Marvin, I'd really like to see you, too. I've missed you. You'll be there tomorrow?" There were already butterflies dancing in her belly.

"Tonight. Come when you can. I'll be waiting."

There was a click and then the hum of the dial tone. Cindy stared at the phone in disbelief. Tonight? That meant that he was already in town. She looked down at herself, dressed in sweatpants and a t-shirt, as well as her housecoat and slippers, clothing for a leisurely evening home alone. Not that she owned anything flashy or sexy, but she could at least make herself somewhat more presentable. Returning the receiver to its resting place, she shoved the newspaper aside and hurriedly struggled to her feet.

Cindy would have to leave a note for Caleb in case she was not back when he returned home. She would simply inform him that she had gone for coffee with a friend. There was no lie in that. Part of her felt guilty for wanting to go in the first place—for wanting to reach out and touch that life that she had thrown away, if only for the length of time it would take her to drink a cup of coffee; the rest of her was exhilarated.

She scurried off to her bedroom, pumped with adrenaline. At the back of her mind was the faintest hope that Mars had come to whisk her away from this death of spirit masquerading as life, and that he would somehow manage to convince her to go.

The coffee shop was only a few blocks from her home and Cindy was beyond nervous, so although it was dark out she decided to walk to shed some of her tension on the way over. She had no idea if he was still the same old Marvin, or if becoming Mars Grimm had changed him significantly. She would know very soon.

The night was chill and she drew in the crisp air in great gulps. It reminded her of the cool but humid environment that night they had walked alongside the lake after the concert in the gazebo. It had been very romantic, and Marvin hadn't broken a single of her father's rules until he leaned forward to kiss her. Cindy brought her fingers up to her lips. A single kiss would have done no harm, rules or no rules, but she had been the one unwilling to leave it at that. Her reaction to him, her responsiveness, had frightened her, and that was what she had really run from, not Marvin.

As she neared the coffee shop, she could pick out the silhouette of someone hovering by the front entrance, someone tall and lean. She wondered if that could possibly be Marvin, and was curious as to why he had not gone inside to wait. Perhaps he was worried that he might be recognized, and draw a crowd —the hometown boy who struck it big returning for a visit. He'd probably have more people flocking to him here than he'd have in LA, fascinated to see the dark, glittery sheep that had strayed from the herd. The town was filled with small-minded people who liked to think small-minded thoughts and gossip was pure gold to them.

That notion gave Cindy a new set of jitters. If someone did recognize Mars, and spotted her with him, word would surely get back to Caleb. Perhaps meeting him in a public place was not such a good idea after all. It wasn't too late to turn back and stand him up. She was barely within earshot, and she doubted he was aware that it was her approaching in the dark, especially not when he appeared to be wearing some sort of fanciful sunglasses that swirled with entrancing green lights—some sort of celebrity goth fashion statement, she guessed, although it seemed more like something you might expect from Elton John's wardrobe. Her heart skipped a beat, fear once again overriding her desire for a brief encounter with the man whom she would always love and secretly long for. She turned to make her escape.

"Don't go."

Cindy froze. That was his voice, although slightly distorted, just as it had been on the phone. He had somehow sensed that it was her. She couldn't just leave now, not without an explanation. She veered about to face him again

"I made a mistake, Marvin. I can't meet with you in a public place. You know how people talk around here. My husband would consider this unforgivable and I'll pay for this little get together for months. I can't stay."

"He'll never know. Come."

His voice softened as he took a few steps towards her and extended his hand in her direction. She still could not see his face properly in the evening shadows, but there was something particularly alluring in that tone he used, especially in conjunction with that pulsating warm green glow that his sunglasses provided. The combination was almost hypnotic, and it struck down that fear that had been about to drive her away, replacing it with renewed desire. Her heart fluttered wildly in her chest, like it had by the side of the lake before they had kissed, and it ignited a fire in her veins—a fire long dead.

Cindy approached him close enough to allow him to grasp her hand, and he began to lead her away. He was not taking her into the coffee shop, however, but pulled her into the alleyway beside it instead. Flustered, and in somewhat of an excited daze, she followed without question. Instead she started blathering incessantly, tripping over her tongue in the rush to get the words out.

"The reason I agreed to meet you, Marvin, was that I wanted to apologize to you for the way I treated you that last year and a half in high school. You didn't deserve that. You were a good friend—I'd hazard to say my only real friend—and I was being insecure." Her mouth was suddenly dry, and her voice cracked. "I blamed you for my own reservations and my own desires running rampant, but that was unfair. It wasn't your fault. I'm not asking for a second chance, since we've both gone our separate ways and you have your music career and I have my family, but I'm hoping at least for forgiveness." She wasn't asking for a second chance, but a tiny part of her desperately wanted one. It was screaming in its shrill little voice, deep inside of her: "Get me out of here! Set me free!"

Mars said nothing at first, but did not release Cindy's hand. She noticed his fingers were unusually cold, even considering the chill moist air, as if she were holding the hand of a dead man. The skin felt a little moist and papery, too. It almost made her own skin crawl. He then began to pull her in closer, as he raised his sunglasses with his free hand.

She had to restrain a squeal of horror, until the mesmerizing effects of what she saw there overrode her senses and numbed all emotion but desire. Thanks to the swirling polka dots and brilliant green lights that pulsated within his eyes, she could no longer fight her attraction to the king of goth rock. It didn't matter that he wore the pale dead flesh of a walking corpse, his face and eyes devoid of any life or soul other then what had burrowed into his brain and eyeballs and was drawing her in with its bizarre lightshow. It had reawakened that yearning within her and that need absolutely demanded to be sated. She closed the gap between then and leaned towards him, hoping he might return the offered kiss. He released her hand and clamped his fingers over her arms, pulling her tight to him with a superhuman vise-like grip. Then he closed his frigid lifeless mouth over her warm, eager lips.

At first, Cindy thought it was his tongue that Mars was wedging with passionate vigor into her mouth, but as she began to choke and gag on the wriggling things that were forcing their way down her throat, she realized that she was sorely mistaken. The discomfort, however, was very temporary. There were only a few moments of panic before the special effects of the specially adapted broodsacs kicked in. Just as it had happened for Mars back at the bistro, a wave of well-being, light-headedness and sensual pleasure washed over her. She had never experimented with drugs or even tasted alcohol, so she had nothing to compare it to, but her mind and body quickly gave in to the need for release and yielded to delightful satisfaction. She vocalized this satisfaction, writhing and moaning in Mars' tight grip.

The chemically-induced euphoria would keep her distracted as the parasites established themselves inside her, boring their way into her brain and eyeballs, just as they had done with Mars Grimm. Then they would set about nullifying everything that was "Cindy" retaining only the memories they needed to pursue their next victim. She would be living in the practical sense, but only to fulfill the needs of the creatures her body hosted. For the most part she would be dead, a zombie kept animated to fulfill a specific purpose.

The pair would now be governed by primal instincts, and maternal instincts are some of the strongest. With Cindy in the lead, they would be driven to venture out to her in-laws' house, in order to "recruit" them and her children, the only other thing that she had cared about while she was alive. After that, what had been Cindy and Mars would be free to head off and wreak their havoc on the goth scene and groupies of LA. From there, it wouldn't take long for the evolved broodsacs to spread, their presence hidden in the dark recesses of the goth clubs and disguised by the fact that their new hosts were already trying to look dead, or rather, undead.

In a sick turn of events, Mars and Cindy had both gotten their wishes. He had wanted only her, and she had wanted only escape from her mundane life. Now they were together again, just as he had wanted, and he had provided a way to "convince" her to run, or in their case stagger, away with him. There would be no more mundane life for her either.

And all that it had required on their part was becoming parasite-infested, mind-controlled zombies, thanks to a single serving of very scary escargot.

ZERO

Quietus

By Christopher Beck

1

It began with the peck of a bird.

2

Langley, VA
Saturday, April 10th
8:43am

The starling sat on the limb of an oak, waiting. It was his usual morning perch; from it, he could see the small pond where a pair of wood ducks, also waiting, drifted lazily, as well as the parking lot. He was hungry and knew that breakfast was on the way.

Two minutes later, Charles Reed pulled into the parking lot. The spring breeze teased the few strands of hair that remained in the middle of his head and lifted the end of his tie when he climbed out of his car. In one hand was his briefcase, in the other a Ziploc bag filled with rainbow colored Goldfish. The starling and the ducks valued Reed's punctuality almost as much as his peers did.

"Morning, you two," Reed said as he stepped over the curb and onto the lush, green grass.

The wood ducks turned towards the sound of his voice and began to quack. The Starling said nothing; it just cocked its head and watched and waited.

"Ready for breakfast I see," Reed said. "I've spoiled you two rotten."

The ducks quacked at him some more. They swam hurriedly to the edge of the pond and walked up onto the shore. Their little tails and little butts wiggled with happiness.

"What would you two do if I ever left this place?"

Quack. Quack.

"You're right; I'm not going anywhere anytime soon."

Reed set his briefcase down and opened the bag of Goldfish. The starling knew the sound just as well as the ducks did. It began to hop from foot to foot as its patience waned.

"Here ya go," Reed said. He dipped his hand down in the Ziploc bag, scooped up some of the multi-colored fish-shaped crackers and tossed them on the ground around the ducks.

The wood ducks quacked in appreciation, and then began to gobble the Goldfish up.

The starling waited for a second, maybe two, after the last Goldfish hit the ground, then hopped off the tree branch and glided over to the pond. It landed on the shore, between the two ducks and began to steal their breakfast.

"Get out of here, you damned cretin."

The ducks flinched at Reed's raised voice but knew he was yelling at the greenish black bird between them. They, too, began yelling at the starling. The starling yelled back. The male wood duck opened his wings and flapped them at the unwelcomed quest. The starling snatched up another cracker, and then flew away. It went back to its perch in the oak, swallowed the cracker, and waited for Reed to throw out the next handful of Goldfish.

"Damn ugly thing," Reed said. He watched the starling fly to the tree and then turned back to the ducks. "They're almost as bad as seagulls. Rats with wings, nothing more, the lot of them."

The ducks quacked in agreement. Reed threw them another handful of Goldfish then glanced as his watch.

"Well, time for me to head in," Reed said. "Enjoy the rest of your breakfast," he glanced over and the starling in the tree, "and keep that one away. See you two Monday morning."

Reed picked up his briefcase, turned, and made for the building. Behind him the starling cawed, without looking back he raised his hand and gave the bird the bird.

At the door he swiped his id card and entered the building.

"Morning, Reed," John Bennett said as he stepped from the spacious security room. He was a burly young black man who looked like he could wrestle a bull to the ground. Two other guards, smaller in stature but just as tough, sat in the security room watching the monitors.

"Good Morning, Bennett," Reed said. He placed his briefcase and the belt and watched as the x-ray machine swallowed it whole. He stepped through the metal detector, no problem, and extended his hand to Bennett. "I see they still haven't shut the heat off."

Bennett took Reed's small hand in his mitt-sized one and laughed. "No, not yet," he said. "You know how the brass is. The days may be warm, but the nights are still chilly. As long as the temp keeps dipping down below sixty, they'll keep the heat cranking."

"Feels like a fricking sauna in here," Reed said. He plucked his briefcase of the belt when the machine spat it back out.

"You don't have to tell me. Most of the people who work here come in complaining about it. Until the nights get warmer, we'll all have to suffer together."

It was Reed's turn to laugh. "At least I'm not the only one. Have a good day, Bennett."

"Thanks," Bennett said, "you do the same."

Reed went down the hall, nodded at man and woman stepping out of the elevator, made a left at the T, and entered the atrium.

As with the rest of the eleven-year-old building, no expense was spared during the construction of the atrium. The seven foot windows, their sills set three feet above the brightly polished floor, were stained glass and made the center room look like a cathedral. Above these windows were six-inch-by-five-foot windows paned with the same colored glass. The various trees, plants and flowers, and the sound of running water in the fountain at the center of the room gave it a vibrant rain forest feel. It was an odd combination, sure, but one that worked rather well.

Jeff Beasley, maintenance worker, stood before one of the giant windows turning the crank that opened the small rectangular window above it.

"Hiya, Beasley," Reed said as he headed across the atrium. He looked up at the other windows and saw they were open.

"Morning," Beasley said.

"I don't think it's going to help much."

"I don't think so either, but at least it's something."

"True. Can't wait till they let you guys turn the air on. Have a good one."

"Thanks," Beasley said.

In the corridor on the other side of the atrium, Reed stopped at the first door on the left, unlocked the door and entered. He set his briefcase next to the desk against the far wall, glanced at his watch, 9:00 on the dot, and plucked his lab coat from the hook on the wall.

3

10:36am

The starling had not gone far after Reed entered the building. It stole some more of the Goldfish from the wood ducks, circled the building, like a buzzard over carrion a few times looking for scraps. It was on its way again to see if the Dumpster had yet to be left open when it found one of the open atrium windows. It landed on the sill and peeked its head in. People bustled around below.

Where there are people, the bird knew, there is always food. It hopped of the sill and glided down to the top of a small tree. Spying nothing to satisfy its greedy hunger, it drifted down to the water fountain for a drink. It dipped its beak, looked around, dipped its beak again and then was startled by a loud cough.

The Starling flew back to the treetop.

***

"What am I looking at, Jefferson?" Reed asked. His eyes were pressed against the lenses of a microscope.

"I'll let Cohen tell you that," Jefferson said. "This is her baby. I was just helping out along the way." He glanced at his watch. "She should be here in a few minutes. Interesting, isn't it?"

Reed zoomed in closer on the petri dish. "Very," he said. "How long has she been working with this?"

"About seven months."

Reed pulled his head back and pinched the bridge of his nose. "This is something special," he said. "I cannot wait to hear what Cohen has to say. But first, I have to empty the bladder."

"I need to use the head myself," Jefferson.

Together they walked out of the lab and down the hall to the bathroom.

***

Someone dropped something and, when the coast was clear, the starling made a nosedive for the object. It landed next to it and gave it a peck. It wasn't food, it was a pencil. The bird voiced its displeasure. It was a stubborn creature, however, and wasn't easily deterred. It hopped along the floor looking for anything it could scavenge.

"Hey, get out of here."

The voice came from behind, but the bird didn't look to see to whom it belonged. It took flight once again. This time it stayed low and went down the corridor past the open door to Reed's lab, past the bathroom Reed and Jefferson had just stepped into. Ahead, a door opened and a person stepped out. The starling turned on a dime and headed back in the direction from which it came. Instead of heading back to the atrium, however, it flew into Reed's lab.

The starling quickly circled the room looking for a way out. Not finding one, it landed on the counter next to the microscope. Cocking its head from side to side, taking in its surroundings, the starling saw the Petri dish.

Curious, the starling used its beak to pull the Petri dish out from under the lens. The thick liquid within rippled when in landed on the counter. A clear, plastic lid kept the contents from spilling out and kept the bird from drinking them. Refusing to be denied, it pushed the Petri dish over the edge of the counter. The dish hit the linoleum floor, bounced up, did half a rotation, and hit the floor again. The lid came loose and the thick liquid began to pool on the floor. The starling, wasting no time, jumped to the floor and began to gobble it up.

When Reed and Jefferson returned to the room, the starling was still there on the floor, pecking at the contents of the Petri dish. For a moment both men were stunned by the sight.

"No, no, no," Jefferson said.

"Goddamn it," Reed said. "Quick, Jefferson, close the door."

Jefferson doubled back to the door but it was too late. They had startled the starling and it zipped passed both of them and out the door. They followed the bird down the corridor to the atrium and watched as it escaped through one of the small, open windows.

"Shit," Reed said. Jefferson agreed.

The starling flew to its original destination—the Dumpster. As it had hoped, one side of the lid was left opened. It landed inside and began to pick at the trash bags.

A short while later the bird's quest for eats was cut short when its body began to convulse. It squawked in pain, and then fell over, dead.

The starling's death was painful, but not everlasting. Twenty minutes after its breathing had ceased and its body sunk down amongst the trash bags, it blinked its eyes. It looked around as if confused, then hopped up to its feet, opened its wings and took flight.

4

Pine Haven, VA
12:00pm
Alison Day sat in the grass playing with her two favorite Barbie dolls. Her mother, Rebecca, was weeding her flower garden alongside the house. Alison's 9th birthday party, which was a little more than a month away, was the topic of conversation between the dolls.

"Are you coming to my party?" the Barbie dressed as a lifeguard asked.

"What party?" said the one clad in a nurse's outfit.

"My birthday party, don't tell me you forgot. I gave you an invitation the other day at school."

"Oh, is that what that was? I put it in my book bag but guess it got lost."

"That's okay. I can give you another if you want to come."

"Yes. I would love to come to your party."

"Great. Here is another invitation. Don't lose it."

"Oh, thank you. I won't lose it."

The two Barbie dolls hugged.

"Mommy," Alison said in her normal voice, not the ones she was using for her dolls. "Can we have a Slip N' Slide at my party?"

"I don't see why not," Rebecca said.

"Yay, thank you," Alison said. She turned her attention back to her Barbie dolls. The one dressed as a lifeguard told the one dressed as a nurse to wear her bathing suit when she came to the party.

Rebecca stood and brushed off her knees. "I've got to use the bathroom, bugga."

"Okay."

"Are you hungry?"

"Not really."

"Alright, but I'm going to fix us some lunch soon."

"Okay, mommy," Alison said.

No sooner had Rebecca walked into the house did the starling show up. Yes, *that* starling. It landed on the fence that surrounded the property and studied Alison with unblinking eyes.

Alison didn't know that the European bird was considered a pest. Nor did she think it was ugly, as most people did. To her it was another bird, not as cute as some, but a nice bird none the less. So, instead of telling it to "get" when she saw it sitting on the fence, she welcomed it.

"Hey, birdy," Alison said. The starling cocked its head at the sound of her voice. "Are you hungry?" She pointed to her right. "If so there is a bird feeder over there."

The starling, showing no fear, flew from the fence and landed on the ground five feet away from Alison.

"I don't have anything for you. The food is over there."

The bird hopped forward a few times and then stopped. Alison had never had a bird come this close to her before. It frightened her slightly, but excited her a lot. She turned to tell her mom to look, and then remembered that she had gone to use the bathroom. When she turned back, the bird was closer. It was now only two feet away.

"Hey," Alison said, "do you want to be my pet? Is that why you're coming so close?"

The starling turned is head from one side to the other.

"Huh? Is that what you want?" The bird hopped closer. "I don't know if my mom would let me keep you." She reached out her hand. The bird was inches from her fingertips. "It's okay, I won't hurt you."

Then the starling lurched forward and quickly pecked Alison on the back of her hand… once, twice, thrice…before she jerked it away with a scream.

"Alison, hunny, are you okay?" Rebecca said as she hurried out of the house. "What happened?"

Alison sat holding her hand limply in front of her. She supported her arm by gripping the wrist with her other hand. The starling stood its ground in front of her. If her mom hadn't come out when she did the bird would have attacked again. "The bird bit me!" she cried. Tears washed down her cheeks.

As if the starling knew it was being talked about, it cawed and took flight. Alison and Rebecca watched it until it was out of sight.

"Here," Rebecca said kneeling down next to her daughter, "let me see."

"It hurts!"

"I know it does, baby."

Rebecca gently took the wounded hand into hers. There were three angry red spots on the back of it, and blood leaked out from two of them.

"It got you pretty good."

"P-please don't touch it!" Alison cried.

"Relax," Rebecca said, "I'm not. But we need to go in and clean it up."

"Are you going to put peroxide on it?"

"Yes."

The idea of peroxide being poured onto her wounded hand intensified Alison's fear and panic, and brought forth more tears.

"No, no, no. Please don't put any on it. It's going to hurt."

"No it's not," Rebecca said. She hated lying to her daughter, but knew that the wounds had to be cleaned. "You don't want you hand to get infected, do you?"

"No."

"Then we have to wash it out with peroxide. Okay?"

"No."

"Okay?"

"But it's going to hurt! It hurt before, when I cut my foot, and it's going to hurt this time, too."

"You'll be fine, bugga. Now let's go take care of this."

Before Alison could protest some more, Rebecca helped her to her feet and guided her to her house, through the mud room, across the kitchen, and into the bathroom.

"Sit on the side of the tub. We'll pour some peroxide on you hand, wash it, and the bandage it."

Alison was still panicked, still trembling, but her breathing had evened some, and her tears weren't coming forth as fast. "I hate that bird," she said. "I was only being nice to it and it bit me; stupid bird."

Rebecca went to the medicine cabinet and grabbed the bottle of peroxide. "I'm surprised it got that close to you. Usually wild birds don't do that."

"Maybe it was someone's pet and it got loose."

"Maybe," Rebecca said, "but I don't think so. I can't say I've ever heard of someone keeping a Starling as a pet." She sat on the tub next to her daughter and uncapped the brown bottle. "Okay, put your hand in the tub."

Alison's body tensed up a little at the sight of the bottle of peroxide.

"It's alright, Alison, it's not going to hurt."

"Yes, it is."

"Alright, maybe it'll sting a little, but that means it is working. That it's getting all of the yucky stuff out. You don't want all those germs and stuff to stay in there do you?"

"No," Alison said.

"Good. Now put your hand over here and we'll get it all out," Rebecca said. "The sooner we get it done, the sooner you can go back out and play."

"I don't want to go back outside. I want to stay in and watch TV."

"That's fine," Alison said. "Hand, please."

Alison presented her hand and her mother poured some of the peroxide onto it. The stinging caused her to hiss through her teeth, but it wasn't nearly as bad as she expected. She watched as her mother tipped the bottle a second time.

"See," Rebecca said with a smile, "I told you you'd be fine. See all those little white bubbles?"

Alison nodded.

"That's the peroxide pulling out the dirt and germs, all the yucky stuff." Rebecca turned on the faucet and adjusted the water until it was warm. "Wash and dry your hands; then we'll bandage you up."

After they finished in the bathroom, Rebecca went into the kitchen to make them lunch and Alison went to the living room to watch TV. She grabbed the remote, sat on the couch and brought the TV to life. After she scrolled through the guide and found a show that captured her interest, she looked around for her two favorite Barbie dolls. They were still outside.

Alison walked over to the window and saw the dolls lying on the ground where she had been playing with them...where she had been attacked by the bird. "Mommy," she called out.

"Yeah, bugga," Rebecca called back from the kitchen.

"My Barbie dolls are still outside, can you go get them for me?"

"No. I'm kind of busy at the moment. You go get them."

"I'm scared.

"It's alright. That bird is long gone by now, it isn't going to hurt you again."

"What about the other birds?" Alison asked as she walked into the kitchen.

"They're not going to hurt you."

"How do you know?"

"I just know," Rebecca said. She was making sandwiches. "What happened out there with that starling was a freak occurrence. I understand why you're scared right now, but there's really no reason to be. The odds of anything like that happening again are slim to none. You're a lot bigger than the birds are and they are scared of you. That's why they always fly away when you get close to them."

"Yea, I guess. But I'm still scared."

"It'll pass, and if you want your Barbie dolls you'll have to go out and get them."

"Can I take Kitten with me?"

"I don't care. Just bring her back in with you."

Alison wasn't a tomboy or a "tough" girl—not that she wasn't tough, she was—but was more of a princess, more of a girly girl, and certain things still scared the shit out of her. The dark was one of those things. On the times when she had to enter a darkened room alone, she would call for her cat, Kitten, and carry her, as if she were a talisman, into said room and turn on the light.

"Kitten," Alison called out. "Come here, Kitten."

The all-white cat answered with a meow, jumped off the chair beneath the table, and padded over to Alison.

"Come on, girl," Alison said as she scooped the cat up, "you're coming outside with me."

The cat was a loveable one, one that craved attention, so it didn't fight or try to get out of Alison's arms. Kitten was used to being carried around, and she rather enjoyed it.

With the cat in her arms, Alison stepped outside. She paused on the steps on other side of the door and cautiously looked around. A hummingbird buzzed around the feeder in the flower bed Rebecca had been working in. When it saw Alison, it flew away. A couple of finches dined at the feeder she had pointed out to the starling. They, too, fled when they saw her. The Starling itself was nowhere to be found.

Good, Alison thought, *stupid bird.* She rushed over to where she had been playing, maneuvered Kitten so her arm circled under her front legs and around her chest, scooped up her Barbie dolls with her free hand, and hurried back in the house. Before she closed the door behind her, Alison heard a caw. To her it didn't sound normal. To her it sounded menacing, evil. She did not look back to see if the starling had returned.

5

1:55pm

A caw brought Alison up out of sleep. She had lain down on the couch after her lunch and, with her two favorite Barbie dolls lying with her, fell asleep.

At first the caw didn't register, she thought, perhaps, the voice belonged to a bird on the TV. When she opened her eyes and looked over at it, however, she saw Carly, Sam and Freddie on the screen, not a bird.

Caw!

Then she remembered the nasty caw she had heard on the way back in the house. This one sounded just like it. Fear swept through her body and she sat up. The back of her wounded had itched beneath the bandage and she scratched at it absently as she scanned the room for the Starling.

Caw!

It came from the direction of the kitchen.

"Mommy," Alison said. It was more of a question than anything.

No response from Rebecca.

Alison snatched up her Barbie dolls and hugged them to her chest. She scratched at her hand again as she stood and a corner of the bandage came loose.

"M-Mommy...?"

Caw!

At the cry of the starling, Alison wanted to turn away from the doorway to the kitchen and run upstairs. Yet it also compelled her to walk forward.

The kitchen was brightly lit by the sunlight. It was empty, but nothing was out of place; all was as it should be. All but the tranquility that is; the caw of the starling had disturbed that. Alison didn't feel safe here as she should. She wanted out of the house, but she could leave, not yet. For some reason she had to find the bird.

Caw!

It came from her left: the bathroom.

She thought about calling out for her mom again then let the idea go. The starling was more important at the moment.

The arm with the bandaged hand held the Barbie dolls to her chest. Alison kept scratching at the bandage as she walked to the bathroom; another corner of it came loose. She paused just outside of the door and listened. All was silent: there was no flutter of wings, no sound of a beak exploring the surroundings, no caw. From where Alison stood, the bathroom seemed just as empty as the kitchen. But it wasn't, she could feel it deep in the pit of her stomach, the starling was in there. She reached in with her scratching hand and flipped on the light. She ducked and shielded her head with her arm, fearing that the bird, infuriated by the sudden light, would come rushing at her. It didn't.

Alison lowered her arm and straightened up. The bathroom *was* empty. Her good hand resumed scratching at the wounded one and the loose end of the bandaged flipped over, exposing the wounds on the back of her hand. Her fingers continued scratching and, with the bandage out of the way, felt something that didn't belong. She looked down and saw what appeared to be thick, coarse, black hairs protruding from the wounds.

Alison's subconscious knew what they were before she did. She took the Barbie dolls in her good hand and lifted the wounded one up to eye level. A chill passed through her body. The closer inspection showed her that protrusions were not hair follicles but tiny feathers.

Without thinking about what she was doing, Alison dropped her Barbie dolls and rushed over to the bathroom sink. She turned the water on and soaped up her hands. She scrubbed the back of her wounded hand vigorously. She rinsed, saw that the feathers were still there, then soaped up and began scrubbing again.

Caw!

The sharp, harsh cry made Alison jump. It came from in front of her. With the water still running and her hands still covered in soap, she slowly raised her eyes to the mirror above the sink. From the shoulders down, her *'flection* was as it should be, from the shoulders down it was her. From the shoulders up, however, it was not. Instead of her small round face, fixed with brilliant emerald eyes and framed by golden hair, the head of a starling stared back at her.

Frozen with terror, Alison couldn't move, but her reflection could and did. Much like the starling that had attacked her earlier, her reflection—part her…part bird—cocked its head at her. Time slowed, the bathroom began to go out of focus. Then her reflection cawed. The room and time returned to normal. Alison screamed—

—and was still screaming when her mother shook her awake.

It wasn't the first time Rebecca witnessed her daughter having a bad dream, and it wasn't the first time she heard her scream because of one. It was normal for it to happen from time to time, and not only with children. Everybody has nightmares. But, it was the first time she had seen her flailing around so violently, and it was the first time she heard Alison let loose such a dreadful, primal scream.

"Alison," Rebecca said, pulling her daughter up in to her arms, "it's okay, baby. Calm down. It was just a bad dream." She held her close and gently rocked her. "Just a bad dream, baby, it's over now. It's over."

Alison, slick with sweat, clung tightly to her mother. Her screaming turned into sobs.

"Okay, baby, it's okay. You're okay."

Rebecca could feel waves of heat pouring out of Alison's skin. She knew it could be because of the nightmare; the trashing about could have raised her body temperature, but she didn't think it was the cause. She knew the difference between a fever and a hot flash.

"Alison, hunny," Rebecca said, "do you feel okay?"

Alison said nothing, but shook her head.

"You feel fevered. You sit here while I go get you some ice water."

"Okay," Alison said weakly. Her mother put her back on the couch and went to the kitchen.

Alison, her train of tears slowing down, picked up her Barbie dolls and hugged them. She thought of her dream and the way her wounded hand had itched in it—and what it was that had caused the itching. If her hand started itching now,while she was awake, she wouldn't scratch it. She would push it down between the cushions, bite her lip and bear it.

Rebecca came back in the living room with a cup of ice water in one hand and the thermometer in the other. "Here," she said handing the cup to Alison, "drink some of this. I'll take your temperature in a few minutes."

Alison took the cup, took a few small sips and set the cup on the end table. "My tummy doesn't feel good, mommy." She took a Barbie in each hand then crossed her arms over her stomach.

"Feel like you are going to be sick?" Rebecca asked.

"Yeah," Alison said.

"You want the trash can?"

"Yes."

The trash can Rebecca was referring to was the small one from the bathroom. Whenever Alison had an illness that involved vomiting, Rebecca would remove the bag from the can, fill it with a small amount of water and place it next to the couch or Alison's bed, depending where she was lying.

Rebecca went to retrieve the trash can and came back with it not a moment too soon. As soon as she set it down, Alison had her face in it. Rebecca sat down, put the towel she had brought with the trash can on the couch next to Alison and began to gently rub her back.

No matter how old Alison grew, no matter how grown up she became, she would always, ALWAYS, be Rebecca's baby. And it would always pain her to see her baby like this. When her baby hurt, she hurt.

Alison's vomiting seemed to last for hours. She pulled her head back, thick lines of saliva hanging from her lips and chin, tears hanging from her eyes, and they both thought she was finally done, but she wasn't. She dipped her head back into the bucket and threw up again.

Poor girl, Rebecca thought. *There can't be anything left in her belly to come out.* She wanted to say something comforting, but knew that words weren't going to help at this point.

The vomiting finally ceased. Alison used the towel to wipe the remnants from her face and sat back on the couch. The look upon her face was a pitiful one

Wearing a frown, Rebecca reached out and began stroking her daughter's hair. "Does your tummy feel any better?" She asked.

Alison nodded and said, "A little."

"That's good," Rebecca said. "Hopefully the worst is over." She took the cap off of the thermometer. "Gotta take you temperature, okay?"

Alison nodded again.

Rebecca brushed the hair away from Alison's ear, inserted the thermometer, pressed and held the button for a second, and then removed it.

"Is it high?" Alison asked.

"A little," Rebecca said looking at the digital read-out, "but not as bad as I thought it would be. You're at 101.2." She put the cap back on the thermometer and stood. "I'm going to empty the bucket and get you some Tylenol. Lay there and rest. Try to drink some more of the water, too, it'll help."

"Okay," Alison said weakly.

Shortly after Rebecca gave her a dose of Tylenol, Alison fell asleep once more. This time, thankfully, it was dreamless.

6

3:32 pm.

Rebecca sat at the kitchen table sipping a mug of hot tea. She was pondering what could have brought on Alison's sudden illness. Her first thought, on account of the vomiting, was that she had eaten something bad. *Could be food poisoning, but we ate the something for breakfast and lunch and I didn't get sick.* Her second thought, on account of the starling attack, was that Alison had contracted the bird flu. *It could explain why the damn bird was acting funny and came up to her like that. But, I haven't heard much about the bird flu lately, and, if she did have it, would it affect her so quickly? Isn't there an incubation period?* She took a sip of her tea. *Maybe I should make a doctor's appointment and have her checked out, just to be on the safe side.*

"MOMMY...!"

Alison's cry startled Rebecca out of her thoughts. Her heart rate instantly doubled. She set the mug down, shoved the chair back, the feet of which screeched in protest as it skidded across the hardwood floor, and hurried to the living room.

"What, bugga?" Rebecca asked as she crossed over the threshold. To say that there was a hint of panic in her voice would be an understatement. "What's wrong?"

Alison was sitting upright on the couch. Her terrified eyes were as big as an owl's. She lifted her arm up in front of her and said, "My hand."

Rebecca took Alison's bandaged hand into hers. She could see that it was swollen and bright red, as if covered in a nasty rash. And the redness didn't stop at her hand; it had climbed over her wrist and up part of her forearm.

"Oh my God," Rebecca said.

"What is it mommy? What's happening?" Alison's voice was no longer just weak, it was weak and pathetic.

"I don't know, baby." She gently touched Alison's red forearm. "Does it hurt?"

Alison flinched and said, "Yeah, some."

"Get your flip flops on; we're going to the hospital."

As Alison did as she was instructed, Rebecca found her sneakers, pushed her bare feet into them and snatched up her purse. Back in the living room, she took hold of Alison's good hand and said, "Let's go, bugga."

"Wait," Alison said, "my Barbie dolls." She tuned back to the couch, picked them up and tucked them under her arm.

The hospital was forty minutes away, but Rebecca was determined to make it there in twenty. Something was wrong—seriously wrong—with her baby and there was no time to waste.

They were out of their small community and in the country, where Rebecca could make haste, in five minutes.

Aside from the humming of the tires, the inside of the car was silent. For some reason the silence unsettled Rebecca. A chill found the back of her neck and made the hairs there stand on end. She tried to rub it away; it was a vain attempt. The radio could break the silence, she knew, but music didn't seem fitting at the moment. So, she tried idle chit chat.

"How are you making out over there?" At the rate of speed she was traveling, Rebecca didn't dare take her eyes from the road.

"I'm scared, mommy," Alison said.

"I know you are, baby," Rebecca said. "Everything's going to be alright. We'll get you to the hospital, the doctors there will figure out what's wrong, and then they'll make you all better."

"Will they give me a shot?"

"I don't know, but it is likely that they will have to give you one."

"No. I don't want a shot. They hurt."

"I know they do, but they also help make people who are sick better."

A few moments of silence passed before either of them spoke again.

"My nose is bleeding, mommy." Alison said.

This got Rebecca to take her eyes from the road. She looked over at Alison who was already looking at her. The sight helped to lower her heart down into the pit of her stomach.

A thin, crimson stream trickled down from Alison's nostril and over her lips. She held her good hand, palm up, below her chin to catch the drippings.

For a second Rebecca was speechless. The bloody nose didn't alarm her as much as how quickly it was flowing did. *My baby is dying.* There was no room for such thoughts and Rebecca mentally reprimanded herself for it. Still, It didn't keep her from thinking that thought over and over again.

"Oh, baby," Rebecca said. She wanted to cry. "There should be some napkins in the glove box. Use them for the blood till we get to the hospital.

"Okay," Alison said. Fresh tears hung heavily in the corner of her eyes. She took some of the napkins from the glove box and pressed them to her nose.

7

4:30pm

Rebecca sat in the hard plastic chair and her leg bounced uncontrollably. Concern wrinkled her forehead. They had only been waiting ten minutes, but to her it seemed like an hour. Her eyes kept wondering to the clock on the wall and it wasn't helping. Try as she might, she could not keep her eyes under control. It was pissing her off.

Alison, with napkins still wrapped around her bleeding nose and her Barbie dolls still tucked under her arm, took in her surroundings. According to her mom she had only been to the Emergency Room once, she had fallen down the stairs five years before and broken her wrist, but it wasn't a visit she could recall. And it wasn't a place she hoped to visit again—ever.

"Mommy…" searing pain gripped Alison's stomach before she could finish. She howled in agony. The dolls and the napkins fell to the floor as she clenched her stomach with both arms.

"Alison!" Rebecca instinctively put her arm around Alison's back.

"It hurts, mommy! It hurts!" Alison pitched over and fell down on the floor between her two favorite Barbie dolls and the bloody napkins.

As soon as Alison tipped forward, time slowed for Rebecca. Wide eyed, she watched as her daughter fell to the floor in slow motion. She let out a yelp and slowly got to her feet. She reached for Alison with hopes of breaking her fall, but didn't make it in time. She watched as Alison hit floor, bounced back up an inch or two, and then thudded against the floor again. She knelt down beside her daughter, their eyes met, and time resumed normal speed.

"Jesus! Alison, are you okay?!" Rebecca said.

Alison went to answer, then her eyes rolled back into her head. She let out a whimper as her body began to convulse.

"Oh, God, someone help!" Rebecca cried out. She wanted to take Alison into her arms but was too scared to do so. "Please! Someone help my baby, she's dying!"

A nurse rushed over, got down on her knees and took hold of Alison's head. "Ma'am," she said, "I know this isn't an easy thing to see, but she needs you to be as calm as you can be."

Rebecca was paralyzed. Tears poured from her eyes but she couldn't move. She heard what the nurse had said, but couldn't respond. The pounding of her heart reverberated in her head. Her breathing hitched.

Another nurse came, slid down onto her knees, opened Alison's mouth and placed a wooden object between her teeth.

Then there was a hand on Rebecca's shoulder, it belonged to another nurse. The touch reinstated her movement. She turned and looked up at the nurse beside her.

"Breathe, ma'am," the nurse said. "We're going to take care of your daughter, but you have to breathe."

Rebecca gasped as if she were taking her first ever breath.

"That's it, ma'am," the nurse said. "Good. Breathe in, breathe out."

Rebecca found breathing to be easier as she focused on and listened to the nurse. She reached up, placed her hand on top of the nurse's and squeezed. The nurse gave her a sympathetic look and squeezed her shoulder in return.

"That's it," the nurse said, "deep, even breaths."

Rebecca nodded at the nurse and then returned her attention to her daughter. In the short time she had been focused on the nurse another had brought out a gurney.

"Alright," the nurse holding Alison's head said, "let's get her on the gurney and into the back."

The nurse who was squeezing Rebecca's shoulder removed her hand and went to join the other nurses around Alison's body.

"Everyone ready?" the nurse at Alison's head asked.

"Yes," the other three said in unison.

"Okay, lift on three; One…two…three."

The four nurses lifted Alison from the floor and gently put her on the gurney. They rushed her out of the waiting room and through double doors to the Emergency Room proper. Rebecca followed.

A doctor, studying records, stood in front of the nurses' desk as the convoy neared.

"We need you, doctor," said the nurse who had taken control.

The doctor glanced at Alison's convulsing body and followed without complaint.

As they neared an empty room, Alison's body became still.

"Is… is she…" Rebecca didn't get to finish the question.

"She stopped breathing," the lead nurse said. "Let's get her in there stat."

They rushed Alison into the room.

"Let's start CPR," the doctor said. He began a rhythmic count as he pressed down on Alison's chest. Without hesitation the lead nurse grabbed a disposable resuscitator and put it over her mouth and nose. She watched the doctor and squeezed it when he said, "breathe."

Rebecca stood in the doorway and watched the scene in horror. Her tears rained down upon the floor.

"It's not working," the doctor said after a few minutes. "Ready the defibrillator." He backed up a step and waited as a nurse took a pair of scissors and split Alison's shirt up the middle. The lead nurse rolled the defibrillator over and he stepped forward and took the paddles in hand.

"Clear."

He put the paddles to Alison's chest and gave her a jolt. The lead nurse checked her pulse. "Nothing," she said.

"Clear."

"Still nothing," the nurse said.

"Clear."

The nurse looked up at him and shook her head.

The doctor sighed and said, "I'm calling it." He glanced at his watch. "Time of death: 4:42pm." He looked over at Rebecca. "I'm sorry, ma'am."

Rebecca was shaking her head. Her mouth was moving but no words were coming out.

"Clear the room," the doctor said. "Let's give her a few minutes."

After the nurses and doctor had left the room, Rebecca slowly walked over to the gurney. Alison looked like she was lost in a peaceful sleep but she knew that she wasn't. Alison was dead, and Rebecca's whole world had just crumbled down around her feet.

"Ma'am...?"

The voice caused Rebecca to jump. She looked to the doorway and saw a nurse standing there with Alison's two favorite Barbie dolls in hand.

"I believe these belonged to your daughter." The nurse stepped forward and handed them to Rebecca.

Rebecca still couldn't speak, so she nodded her appreciation.

"I'm so sorry," the nurse said, then turned and fled the room.

Rebecca sat on the edge of the gurney and studied Alison for a moment. She bit her lip to keep from crying out. She put the Barbie dolls on the pillow, one on each side of Alison's head, and then kissed Alison's forehead.

Then Alison's head jerked to the side. The spastic movement caused Rebecca to jump back. Alison's head jerked again.

Was it possible that the doctor and the nurses had been wrong? Was it possible that Alison had fallen unconscious and was not dead? As the questions circled around inside of Rebecca's head, hope started to revive her heart.

"A-Alison...?"

Alison became still once again.

"Alison, baby, can you hear me?"

No response.

She leaned forward and put her ear to Alison's nose. She could not hear any breathing. Her new found hope wilted; she was foolish to think the hospital workers were wrong.

Rebecca sat up and saw that Alison's eyes were open. Only they weren't Alison's eyes, not really. They were black instead of the normal emerald color, and cold instead of warm. Rebecca was suddenly filled with dread. She felt that she needed to get out of the room and quickly. Before she could move, however, Alison's arms reached up and grabbed a hold of her. It was not a loving embrace.

Rebecca screamed.

Alison bared her teeth with a nasty snarl, then shot forward and sunk them into her mother's neck.

MORE TITLES AVAILABLE FROM
MAY DECEMBER PUBLICATIONS

The unthinkable has happened. The dead are walking!
Humanity's fragile thread may be reaching its bitter end.
Individuals and groups struggle to survive…some at any cost. Will there be anybody left?
Or, is this just…

The Ugly Beginning?

See the world through Steve's eyes as he tries to balance the duties of leading a band of survivors while caring for a young, Hispanic orphan girl. Ride along with a band of self-professed "zombie-geeks" who are discovering that living through the apocalypse is vastly different than watching it on television. Peek in at horrifying snapshots of men and women…good and bad. This is—

DEAD: REVELATIONS

(Book 3 available in December)

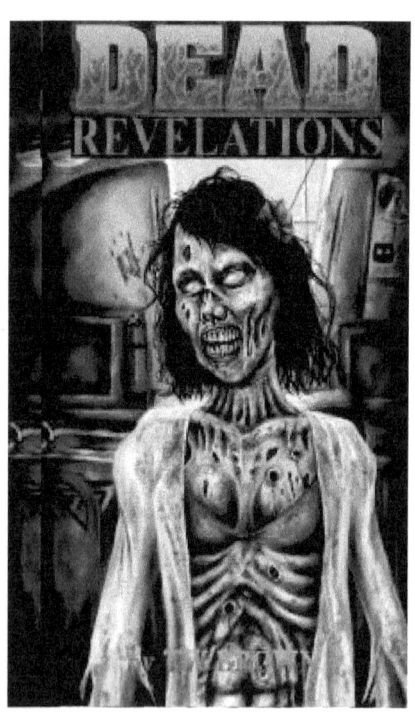

THE DEAD WALK!

Samuel Todd is a regular guy:
...Failed husband...
...Loving father...
...Dutiful worker...
...Aspiring rock star.
He had no idea if anyone would care, or take the time, to read his daily blog entries about his late night observations. But what started as an open monologue of his day-to-day life became a running journal of the first-hand account detailing the rising of the dead and the downfall and degradation of mankind...

Meredith Gainey is a survivor...and determined to retain that status as the zombie apocalypse wipes out most of humanity. Unable to accept an existence behind walls and fences, she finds herself in constant danger...and she wouldn't have it any other way.

The legions of the undead continue to grow. First Time Dead proudly presents a host of brand new names to the genre pantheon. Each writer contained herein might be the next "it" writer on the rise…the one to watch for. You never know where the next Romero, Kirkman, Brooks, Keene, or Wellington may emerge to scare and entertain the masses.

Our matched set anthologies
Available Mother's Day and Father's Day 2011

It has been said that women are the "gentle" sex. Apparently, not all of them got the message. Within the pages of this anthology are a dozen zombie tales by women who will help you discover why they say something else about the ladies: **Hell Hath No Fury…**

"Ladies first" So say the gentlemen.
This is the companion anthology to Hell Hath No Fury…Inside, you will find an undead bakers dozen that will remind you of how dark and desolate the minds of men can truly be. Vowing not to be upstaged by the dark musings of their female cohorts, the men offer up a usceral, gore-drenched collection that strives to prove… **Chivalry is Dead**

Slip into the skin of common men and women and experience the horror through their eyes. Follow the Zombie Apocalypse from its initial stages to the brink of the abyss, and over…into the pits of an unthinkable Hell on Earth. Tune into your local radio stations for the latest updates or stay here and follow the story as it unfolds on…

Eye Witness: Zombie

MayDecPub.com/ *e*-LIT

MAY DECEMBER
Publications

The growing voice in horror and speculative fiction.

Find us at www.maydecemberpublications.com

Or

Email us at contact@maydecemberpublications.com